MW00587034

THE
WOMAN
IN THE
TREES

THEONI BELL

TAN Books
Gastonia, North Carolina

Copyright © Theoni Bell, 2020

No part of this book may be reproduced or transmitted in any form by any means—electronic, mechanical, photocopy, or otherwise—including information storage and retrieval systems, without permission in writing from the author, except by a reviewer who may quote brief passages in a review.

Disclaimer: This story is loosely based on actual events. Some characters and timelines have been changed for dramatic purposes. Certain characters may be composites or entirely fictitious. The roles played in this narrative by Adele Brise, Xavier Martin, Reverend Peter Pernin, and Reverend Edward Daems are entirely fictional. Their conversations, letters or thoughts have no factual basis. My imagined Brise, Martin, Pernin, and Daems do, however, abide by the generally known facts of their real lives.

The story of the kabouters is a Dutch fairy tale that was taken from the book "Dutch Fairy Tales," by William E. Griffis, 1918.

Editing by Kathryn Hnatiuk and Carolyn Astfalk.
We gratefully acknowledge the following institutions for permission to reproduce the photographs in this book: photograph of Adele Brise from the archives of the Sisters of Saint Francis of the Holy Cross in Green Bay, WI, and photograph of stained glass window at St. Stanislaus Church, Milwaukee, WI, from its creators at Conrad Schmitt Studios.

ISBN: 978-1-5051-2378-4
Kindle ISBN: 978-1-5051-2379-1
ePUB ISBN: 978-1-5051-2380-7

Cover Design by Chris Lewis (www.barituscatholic.com)

Visit www.TheoniBell.com

Published in the United States by
TAN Books
PO Box 269
Gastonia, NC 28053
www.TANBooks.com

To Mary,
for whom I tried to write well.

For my oldest daughter, MRB.
This novel wasn't ready until you read it.

To my whole family,
sorry I'm a bit of Mrs. Lafont at times.
I love you.

CONTENTS

THE
WOMAN
IN THE
TREES

CHAPTER ONE

Fire

1871

SLAINIE LAFONT SHOT up in her bed. She blinked until the dark came into focus. Outside, a goat brayed wildly. She could identify all the animals in a tumult. Chickens squawked and growled. The guttural lowing of cows rang out. Hogs squealed.

Throwing off her quilt, she rushed to the cabin's kitchen window. *Smoke!* In the distance, flames rose above the shadowy peaks of pines, glowing orange. Plumes of smoke spread as if engines were barreling through the woods, sending up mountains of steam as they chugged toward her. It wouldn't be long before that smoke, and its fire, reached her little log cabin. Slainie shook her husband Joseph awake and yelled across the house to rouse their daughters. Odile shuffled down from the loft. In dim candlelight, she watched her mother with tired eyes.

Slainie threw open the bread bin. She grabbed at provisions from several cabinets, unconsciously muttering the name of each as she jammed them into a sack. "Venison . . . butter mold . . . the last of the loaf." Suddenly, she swung around. "Odile!" The little girl jolted out of her midnight stupor. "Go grab some clothes!"

Darting frantically around the cabin, Slainie thrashed drawers and baskets, whittling her belongings down to a list of bare necessities. "Blankets . . . coats . . . lantern . . . baby clothes." When she was done, she scrambled across the wood floor, throwing her sack by the front door.

Slainie noticed her five-year-old daughter still watching from the hallway. "Odile, I told you to go! Gather some smocks. Bring them to me."

Odile didn't flinch. With a blank stare, she stood frozen.

Thrusting an arm toward Odile's room, Slainie shattered her daughter's bewilderment. "Odile, go now!"

"Mama, what are you doing?" Odile's voice was low and shaky.

"I'm packing . . . please do as I say." There was no time for Slainie to explain to Odile why they were packing and then answer questions about it. She didn't want to terrify her daughter either.

Odile took her one-year-old sister by the hand. They shuffled halfway across the parlor. Slainie called out, "Leave Sophie with me. You hear? You must move quickly. Now! Quickly!"

As Odile climbed to the loft, Slainie stretched her arms under couches and tables searching for shoes: hers, her husband's, Odile's, and little knitted booties for Sophie. She caught sight of the smoke billowing outside the window.

Slainie's husband, Joseph, came limping in from the hallway. "Here's our clothing." Slainie plucked the bundle from his arm and jammed them into her sack. Grimacing, Joseph hurried off again, his permanent war disabilities threatening to slow him down.

Slainie ran toward the loft.

"Odile? Just throw some clothes down—we must leave."

Baby Sophie crawled into Slainie's sack by the door. Candlelight flickered on her soft, round face as she pulled at the buttons of a sweater. Noticing Sophie there, Slainie stopped abruptly.

Where are we going to take you?

Suddenly, Joseph drew Slainie into a corner, turned his back to Odile and lowered his voice. "We need to get to water, Slay. We don't have long before the fire's here."

"I know. I am trying to place any streams or ponds near us. Even a well would do. Certainly, we can't reach the bay. The fire is coming from that direction."

"Yes, then, a well or a stream. We need it to be close."

Outside, something popped in the distance, and Joseph hurried to the door, flinging it open. They coughed as smoke invaded the room. A cloud of gnats fluttered in, propelled by a gale.

Joseph swiped the bugs from his face. "What do you make of that?"

Slainie listened intently. A loud *crack, crack, crack* echoed in the forest.

"I don't know."

She had never before heard the sound of trees crackling—as if screaming—while flames consumed them, or the sound of a fire creating tornadoes as it sucked up all the air, or the force of scorching whirlwinds thrashing hundreds of trees at a time. But she knew it immediately.

"It's coming, Joseph. We must go."

"We need to get my parents and Henri. Then we run." As Joseph spoke, Sophie climbed into his good arm and clung to his shirt with her little fists.

"Yes, by all means." Slainie pulled Odile to the door, sharing a horrified look with Joseph. The smoke unfurled across the sky above them.

Joseph nudged Slainie to hurry down the porch steps. Her mind raced to all the places she knew on that little arm of Wisconsin—the mills, the villages, the streams, the port, and the churches. *Where can we go?* Lake Michigan was on the other side of the peninsula, but it was too far away to be a refuge for them. It would take all night to get there, if the fire didn't overrun them first. Suddenly, her thoughts slowed to a single image. A woman with flowing black robes stood at the door of a chapel. She recognized the figure at once—Adele Brise, that mysterious and revered teacher. In the image, flames danced around Adele, but she stood serenely, paying no attention to the fires that threatened to consume her. *What does this mean?*

Joseph jostled past, trying to carry Sophie and move Odile along with his knees. Snapping out of her daze, Slainie followed. A wagon charged by. Though barely visible in the dark, the crack of a whip on horseflesh resounded above the fire's roar. Something large, like a barrel, bounced off the back, and cries cut through the acrid air—the neighbors' children wailing.

"That's Emma, Josephine and baby Nicolas." Odile grabbed Slainie's hand, pulling her toward the road. "Look, Mama, someone is burning trees again. Look at the sky."

Without responding, Slainie tugged Odile backward and started running with Joseph as fast as she could. She turned her head to catch one final glimpse of her home. Then, she made for the home of Joseph's parents, who lived on the other side of the wheat field. Slainie prayed that they were awake. She prayed they'd be right there, at the door, ready to flee. Then her mind came back to the question, *where are we going to go?*

CHAPTER TWO

Knock, Knock

1859 / 12 years before the fire

THE CABIN WHERE Slainie lived as a child sat in the center of a hard-won clearing. For thousands of years, a forest of conifers and broad-leaved trees had grown unhindered in that spot. Some of those trees were as thick as four feet across. Only Indians had traversed there. In 1853, the Belgian settlers arrived, and with them, Slainie Lafont.

In those early pioneering years, the settlers hacked and sawed unceasingly at the forest. They had no use for the amount of trees they felled, so each day smoke from mountainous piles of burning logs permeated the sky. Now, stumps studded the ground where trees once stood. Some of those stumps still squatted near the Lafont family cabin, while the rest had been wrestled from the earth. In their place, the now-plowed soil was home to a few hogs and a garden of squash, herbs and spindly flax plants.

Twelve-year-old Slainie foraged a ten-minute walk from her cabin. She zigzagged over a burbling stream, a quicker route than the trails, with a basket swaying in the crook of each arm. Skirts wet in the autumn breeze, she raced home shivering.

Something else tugged at her mind, hastening her steps; the new edition of *Frank Leslie's Illustrated Newspaper* awaited her. A giant coal-powered ship was splashed across the cover. Detailed hordes of people amassed on the wharf beside it. Slainie couldn't read, but *Leslie's* covers—wood engravings painted with ink and stamped on the page—always thrilled her. They usually depicted tragedies. The last edition of the newspaper to circulate among the settlers featured a rioting crowd. The one before that, an etching of a factory fire. But, prior to that, a poised, proper-looking couple peered out at her—long waistcoat, pocket watch, and lace hemming on a wide-rimmed skirt. They wore all the things important people wear. Slainie admired them, even though she was unable to read who they were.

The November 1859 edition beckoned to her, but she couldn't even turn the cover until she found a break between chores. So, Slainie bounded home, hoping to steal a few minutes of pleasure. When her bare feet landed on a soft patch of grass, she planted them and leaned against the stream bank. After combing her wild, dark hair with her fingers, she twisted it into a bun and tied her black bonnet around her head. She had to tidy up before arriving home.

Slainie had tossed bunches of purple grapes into her baskets without removing all the stems. She had pulled garlic mustard without cleaning the clumps of soil from its roots. The wild onion she'd picked had mixed with the bed of grass cradling her blackberries. None of it would pass her mother's inspection.

On the level ground at the top of the slope, she neatly sorted her bounty. It had been a good trip. She had scavenged more than the usual amount, even in her haste. She placed grapes, berries, onions, and herbs back into her baskets, ready to continue when a *hum* sounded nearby. Climbing the slope, she spotted bees bumbling and buzzing around a low-hanging hive.

Slainie thought of her newspaper. She wanted to dive into its illustrations of life in busy places, like Chicago, Philadelphia, and New York City. But here, in these woods, she had a chance to exceed her mother's expectations. She could bring home many months of honey in that hive. She just needed to kindle a small fire, smoke the bees out and whack their hive from the branches. Then, she could wrap it up and carry it home in her apron.

She stepped closer and scanned the ground for a large stick. This was a big one. The hive hung at least three-feet long and looked like a wet quilt casually flung across the branches, except that the whole thing writhed and waved as the swarm of bees crawled all over each other. A shiver went up Slainie's neck, as she remembered to exhale. It was terrifying.

No, she couldn't whack it down. It looked too much like a hairy swamp creature, the mass of it clinging to the branches as if it were alive. At least she could show her father where it was. *He* could hack it down with her two brothers. She couldn't. Maybe if she had an ax . . . she just couldn't without an ax.

Slainie arrived home just before lunch. She climbed the pegs to her bunk and took hold of her newspaper, admiring the masthead illustration at the top, the tiny detailed columns and domes of the Washington Capitol building in Maryland. She imagined the important business taking place inside.

Too soon, the summons came. "Slainie, meet me in the parlor."

Slainie crawled over to the shelf that ran the length of the loft. Quickly flipping through the magazine, she found an image of a young girl with a parasol and an impressive bow on the back of her bodice. Slainie ripped it out, careful to include a few other people in the park and the thriving flower garden at which the girl was staring.

Reaching for a small tin of tree sap, Slainie glanced at the opposite end of the loft. Above her sister's bed, on Modette's end of the shelf, was a beautifully monogrammed pillow. Red thread swooped into the letters "M" and "L." Every time she saw the rusted thimble sitting next to it, Slainie envied the fact that her mother had given it to Modette. Their grandma had used it back in Belgium, and deep down Slainie knew Modette deserved it. The six-year-old was a sewing prodigy.

Prying a twig from the sap in her tin, Slainie put a dab on the back of the little magazine girl. She pressed the image onto the bare wood of the loft ceiling and leaned back on her hands to survey all the images she prized. The little girl fit right in with all of the other children Slainie had torn from *Leslie's* magazine. She slid the current edition under the shelf, straightening the pile of magazines before she climbed down to answer her summons.

Her mother, Margot Lafont, sat near the fireplace, holding a needle and a piece of linen. Slainie slumped into the chair across from her. A tapping sounded from the door, barely audible. Motionless, Slainie gazed across the room, waiting for the sound to return. *How odd!* Uninvited neighbors visited often, but they usually walked up with a friendly shout. This was only a slight tapping on the wood. When the knock came again, Mrs. Lafont rose from her chair, setting her sewing needle on the wobbly, wooden side table. The heavy door creaked open, and Mrs. Lafont straightened her scarf over her hair when a cool breeze invaded the room.

"Do I know you?"

"Peace to you. My name is Adele Brise." The voice outside was assertive, but tender.

With her mother blocking her view, Slainie couldn't see the woman. She slid her chair to the left as quietly as she could, then leaned over the side. Tipping even further, she finally glimpsed the bottom of a long, dusty black cloak. Her mother shifted, and

Slainie spotted a black cape-bonnet, and under it, the woman's face. She gasped. The right eye socket was sunken, the lid and lashes, all of it. *The eye is missing!* It was just a hole. A ghastly black hole.

Slainie shot out of her chair. "I'll start the tea," she announced. Stumbling on an uneven floorboard, she clambered across the room toward the cooking stove. Adele asked if she could teach the catechism to any children in the home. Slainie had never heard of "catechism" before. She got the hint her mother had, because when Slainie glanced over her shoulder, Mrs. Lafont was grasping the door as if she were preparing to slam it in Adele's face.

"I have only come to offer my assistance . . . and to provide an education in the faith to any child I am able." Adele clutched a leather-bound book in her hands.

Slainie's mother stepped back a little, and Slainie braced for the door to slam.

Adele quickly added, "I only mean, I'm available to help with household chores in return for time with the children. I wouldn't intrude upon the normal operations of your home."

After putting the kettle on the stove, Slainie leaned on the dinner table to watch. Staring down at her calloused hands, her mother seemed to consider the strange offer, but instead tightened them into fists.

"The catechism? But you're not a priest. Shouldn't a priest be doing that, in a church somewhere?" She didn't wait for Adele to respond. "It doesn't matter. My children have no time to donate to wastefulness."

Mother's tone was scathing, and Slainie feared she was eavesdropping on the whole thing. She'd felt a strong urge to apologize to Adele, but that missing eye so shocked her. Grabbing a dish rag, she scrubbed at the table, wondering where Adele's eye had gone. When the kettle whistled, she moved the steaming tea to a flat stone on the counter. Obviously, her mother wasn't offering any hospitality.

In the doorway, Adele stepped forward a little. She began to bid them an odd sort of farewell. "Bless you," she said and made a hand motion in the air.

Slainie's mother shut the door while Adele still motioned above her head. Then she picked up her needle and resumed working on a winter coat.

Slainie strode back to her chair. "What does that woman want to teach us?"

"Oh, I remember the highfalutin Catholics like her in the old country. They think religion has *all* the answers. The Church never helped us." Mrs. Lafont stabbed the needle into her coat, tugging it roughly on the way out. *Stab, tug, stab, tug.* "That woman! She thinks, 'I attend church, so should everybody.' There's no church around here for miles."

Slainie knew not to speak, even though she had so many questions. *Is that woman from the settlement? Why haven't I seen her before? Shouldn't we offer her some food before she walks back from where she came?*

"Don't pay her any mind." Mrs. Lafont tore into her basket of cloth, flinging pieces aside until she found a long panel of deerskin and thrust it across her lap. "For goodness' sakes alive, you're only twelve. You've enough to fill your time. I hear this winter's going to be bad, worse than ever. You worry about that. We're going to be quite hungry when spring arrives."

Slainie knew she couldn't speak honestly with her mother. Suffocated by their mother's constant worry and dark moods, the Lafont children rarely had a break from daily chores or Mrs. Lafont's militant voice directing the completion of them. If their mother did have a moment to relax, she used it to prepare for the coming season, never wasting a moment in serendipitous chatter.

It had been seven years since Slainie's family immigrated to America, and the question remained: Had life been better in Belgium than it was in the Wisconsin wilderness? Slainie could barely remember their hut in Wallonia, but at least back home, if times were hard, her father could scrounge up work in the city. Here, the lack of people made hard times much grimmer. Life in America sounded so simple then: cheap land, easy life. This was not so. America was nothing like they expected it to be.

It seemed like a lifetime ago that six-year-old Slainie first saw the pamphlet that convinced her mother to leave Belgium. One evening, her neighbor Martin Descamps had waved it around the village bake oven. He'd pushed that pamphlet under his neighbors' noses all through supper, hoping to convince them to emigrate to Wisconsin and change their fortunes.

"Look here. It says, 'COME! Opportunities are unlimited for those who want to work.' See, that's us. Picture yourself working your own land instead of going down into these mines or begging for work in the market." Mr. Descamps stabbed his pork sausage and tore off a bite.

"What work?" Mr. Baudin hollered from inside his hut. "Foreigners take all the work in Wallonia."

Slainie's mother wiped her hands on her apron and grabbed the tattered pamphlet. Custard pies bubbled in the brick baking chamber next to her. As she leaned nearer to the fire, her face shone white under her brown cap. She mumbled the words she read, so as not to wake the sleeping baby on her back.

"Come. In Wisconsin all men are free and equal before the law. Religion is free and equal between church and state. Good land can be purchased from the generous American government for $1.25 an acre."

Slainie leaned over her mother's shoulder to hear what the pamphlet promised. "Where's America, Maman?"

"It's a lifetime away. Through the British Sea and across the Great Western Ocean."

Her mother paused, looking thoughtfully at the paper. Wiping sweat from her forehead, she placed a fresh loaf of bread in a bag and handed it to Mr. Descamps. "Are there ships ready to take us?"

"We have heard so, but we haven't met anyone yet leaving," replied Mrs. Descamps.

When nothing but embers glowed in the oven, the villagers collected their children from a nearby fire-pit where they had been playing. Thistles from a bush covered Cecilia, Slainie's four-year-old sister. The little one trudged over with their two older brothers, Jacques and Vincent, as the boys tore thistles from her bottom, bursting with laughter. Mrs. Lafont shook the hand of each of her neighbors, and everyone ambled toward the thatch-roof huts that encircled the communal kitchen.

After Cecilia was nestled into bed, Slainie crawled onto the straw mattress next to her. She waited for the rapid tapping on the door which signaled her father's return from the coal mines. They had expected him earlier that evening. As soon as Slainie heard the long iron rod slide over the door latch, she breathed deeply and peeked out of her blankets. Mr. Lafont lowered his head to enter their one-room hut. Now, Slainie could sink peacefully into sleep—until she heard her father hacking so loudly baby Modette was stirred to wailing. He lit a candle for Mrs. Lafont, who paced with the baby in the narrow space between the beds.

"Your cough hasn't improved."

Mr. Lafont sat on a small bench and tugged his thread-bare boots off. "*Bonsoir, mon chérie.* Good evening, my dear. Yes, it worsened. I have been hewing stones underground for two weeks."

Wasting no time, Mrs. Lafont read him the pamphlet about

America. Curious and attentive, Slainie lay motionless waiting for his response.

"You trust a piece of paper? Did you talk to Adelaide or Martin or Frederic about it?"

"Martin gave it to me tonight. I believe it speaks true, and I want to go. You cannot sustain us here. I'm weaving rugs, neckerchiefs, and undergarments. But *now* the train brings in cheaper linen. Gorgeous, dyed, embroidered—so many embellishments for the price of a plain smock! I cannot find patrons."

"My whiskey should be fermented by summer. The boys should have been running cold water around the barrels while I was—"

Mrs. Lafont cut him short with a curt whisper. "Have you *tried* the whiskey that comes off the train?" She laid the sleeping baby back in their bed.

Slainie's father sighed. "I'm hungry."

"There's pie and a few bits of pork on the table." Mrs. Lafont laid her hand on his shoulder. "Don't you want to give your sons more than this? As it stands, they will inherit a landowner who treats us as swine, who cuts down our plot of land year after year. Our field is no bigger than a garden now. And, if there be another crop famine? No wheat again. No potatoes. No rye."

Mr. Lafont swallowed hard. "*Mon amour.* My love. Please, let us talk tomorrow. Our neighbors may hear and awaken."

Mrs. Lafont jerked her hand back. "I think you're frightened. That's all." She wedged into bed next to the baby. "I will find others who are ready to leave. Maybe they can give you courage."

Slainie smiled under her covers. Knowing her mother's stubbornness, they'd likely be leaving. She imagined vast, open American spaces—meadows and beaches untouched by people.

The next morning, though the larder wasn't empty, Slainie's mother took her children to the village for potatoes and flour.

That pamphlet and others like it were plastered all over town. Every time Mrs. Lafont spotted a new one, she read it to Slainie and her brothers. *American land is beautiful and made of good soil. There is land as far as the eye can see, just waiting to be claimed.*

"Wouldn't you children like to see it?" Mrs. Lafont handed copies of the pamphlet to each of them. Baby Modette chewed on hers for a minute and then threw it in the road.

Slainie's mother spoke to anyone she could—the butcher, the grocer, the women at her sewing club—anyone who could give her the names of other Walloons who were leaving. She clutched the idea of America like the prized schooner ticket that would take her there.

A few weeks later, at the bakeoven, Mr. Descamps pored over a newspaper advertisement from the Strauss Shipping Company. They had printed a testimony from Belgians who had already made the trip to America. *In Belgium, you will always be unhappy, where in America your happiness is in your hands. Here you will eat white bread all the days of your life.* Slainie listened eagerly while playing with Cecilia and Modette in the dirt at her mother's feet. After supper, her father sent the children to their hut.

Climbing into bed, Slainie shushed Cecilia and perked up her ears. Their father spoke quietly outside.

"Listen, the people have America fever, even down in Namur—"

"Cilia!" Slainie had turned and smacked right into Cecilia's forehead. "Why are you creeping up on me? Move over and go to sleep."

With a sly smile, Cecilia inched even closer. "Have you ever seen a kabouter?"

Slainie inched closer to the edge on her side of the bed.

Cecilia followed her. "I saw one this night. Outside, near the garden . . . just behind the rise and in the bushes."

"Be quiet, so I can hear papa," Slainie whispered.

"But I saw him." Cecilia was sitting up now, hovering over Slainie's face. "He was all black with dirt and so tiny. He was cute." She giggled and continued in a low, excited voice. "The kabouter just finished making the bells, and he was actually the *sonnerie de cloche*, the bell ringer."

Frustrated, Slainie pulled Cecilia's legs out, forcing her sister to lay down.

"You know that story is as old as the earth." Slainie took a deep breath. "Okay, here you are. The kabouters are gnomes who live underground and they sound like angels when they sing and they help people who are kind. They work so hard even kabouter mothers and babies are covered in soot. And they hate lazy people. They will trick you. They will get you into trouble if you are mean and lazy."

Listening, Cecilia finally stopped fidgeting and pulled the blanket under her chin.

"In our lands, people used to be bad and mean, but new people came and taught them how to have manners and how to take care of each other. Soon, the people built their first church, but they had no metal to make bells. So the kabouters, who are very happy to help when people are good, mined for metal deep in the earth and built bells of many sizes …."

At the sound of her father's voice, Slainie stopped. She realized Cecilia was asleep, breathing softly beside her. She could finally listen to her parents talking outside.

"Just this week, I was at the market with the miners when I heard the bells ring at Sint Aubain's. When I entered the church, the priest was speaking all about this America fever."

"And, what does our great Church say?" Her mother's indignant tone carried through the night air.

"Father says we mustn't leave. We must stay, because workers are swarming into Wallonia. I believe it—I've seen them. And, these workers don't live like Belgians. They've started a movement, he says, a movement to give charge of all the schools to the government. If the Church loses the schools, the Belgian government will even hire teachers who aren't Catholic."

With the little ones breathing softly beside her, Slainie heard the thud of Mrs. Lafont plunking down on a bench. "Our children aren't going to school."

"They ought to. They will. Truth is, we need to keep together with our folk. We need to fight for our country. The Church should be educating us, not the government."

"If we leave, our children won't be here anyhow. What would we care for the outcomes of politics and revolutions? In America, we're free."

"That's what I'm coming 'round to. What is there for our children in the wild? There'll be no churches, no schools where we're going. We leave and our children will suffer. *And* we'll be no good to everyone suffering these troubles here without us."

Mrs. Lafont's voice rose. "You go to church once a moon and come home preaching? Is religious ignorance the only form of suffering you see? What about achy knees, empty bellies, and children who'll leave us for better somewhere else. As soon as they're grown, they'll all leave us."

Heavy regret sounded in Mr. Lafont's voice. "I can't get to church as often as I wish. I'm only . . . always working."

"In any case, going to church doesn't do us any good. Those bishops sit in their palaces, while we sit in the dirt. They don't even see us."

"You know that's wrong. We've been given bread and clothing from the St. Vincent Society in town. Good folks there."

Voices murmured far off in other huts. Slainie heard the *crunch, crunch* of soil under foot. Then Mr. Jossart's voice rang out firmly. "We could hear you over in our hut, and we wanted to tell you *we're* leaving."

"What?" Mr. Lafont's voice came high and sharp.

A second neighbor's voice chimed in. "That's right. We're leaving, too."

So it happened that Slainie's father found his courage and her mother was happy. Slainie's neighbors already knew of other Wallonians preparing to leave. In the fall of 1853, the Lafont family joined them on the sea voyage to America. A month later, Slainie became an American pioneer.

Since then, Slainie and her now-six-year-old sister Modette had been laboring and keeping house with their mother deep in the Wisconsin woods. Slainie was bone-weary, and the work was monotonous. Drudgery. Were she able to go to school, Slainie would have used these words to describe her life, but she hadn't learned them yet.

After Adele left, Slainie wished the strange visitor had stayed. She wished her mother had accepted the help. Yet, Mrs. Lafont wouldn't accept anything from anyone, especially if it meant she had to endure religion of any kind. She always said a priest follows a "fool's call." Slainie had never seen her mother more annoyed than when a religious person spoke with her about religion, unless of course, that person was also smiling self-assuredly while she spoke.

The small wooden crucifix that hung from Adele's neck made Slanie curious to see the one Mrs. Lafont hid in the bottom of her sewing box. Where had it come from, and why did her mother keep it if she hated the faith so much? Rather than inquire, Slanie responded with an endearing name for her mother, one she had learned to use when her mother was upset.

"I understand, *Maman*. I won't ask any more questions."

CHAPTER THREE

The Teacher

1859 / 12 years before the fire

SLAINIE GAZED OUT the window as the black-clad figure of Adele reentered the woods. Her thoughts drifted. Her own life was so humdrum, she had leapt from her chair at the chance to do nothing more than offer tea to a stranger. But her mother already didn't like this stranger. With her needle teetering on her fingertips, she soon slipped into a slumber. The sound of Mrs. Lafont rummaging in her sewing box startled Slainie awake, and she quickly searched her chair for the needle she had dropped.

Squinting, Mrs. Lafont tied off some white thread. "This is why you don't improve. Let go of your daydreams. You must be accustomed to this life by now." Without looking up from her work, Mrs. Lafont jabbed her hand toward the door. "Since you are no good here, go to the stream for water and see to the garden."

Slainie did what she was told, and returning, was granted permission to visit a friend.

There were only two places Slainie ever walked alone. The first was the Allard family farm, a half-hour hike from home. Slainie made a delivery of clothing there every few weeks. All six of the Allard children—Henri, Marguerite, Zoe, Joseph, Jacques, and Leon—helped in the family's wheat fields, working constantly so their wheat could be delivered to towns around Wisconsin on the new railroad line.

The second place was to her best friend Marie Martin's house. As Slainie walked, she always remembered the nights she had spent at Marie's house in Namur, Belgium. However, now, instead of racing through crowded city streets, she strolled down one of Wisconsin's old Indian trails. The trail continued far beyond the Martins' house and connected with miles and miles of trails that Slainie had never seen. She could have hiked them all the way to the end of the peninsula, fifty miles north.

Seizing the residue of past excitement, Slainie embraced the memory her first trip to Marie's house six years ago. She could almost see the tall rowhouses of the city in front of her. To get to Marie's house back then, Slainie and her family trekked a hilly dirt road through a cultivated countryside. The first time they went, Slainie tugged Cecilia by the arm for hours, impatient to reach the city. Cecilia lifted her little legs to run with all her might. She didn't lack energy, just leg length, and she kept getting distracted.

"No picking flowers, Cilia!" Swiping another handful of grass from Cecilia's hand, Slainie wished she could tie her sister to her back, but Cecilia had grown too heavy for that.

Slainie's first trip to Namur was also her easiest, because about halfway to the city a farmer offered the Lafonts a ride in his wagon. It was suppertime when they set foot on a cobblestone street, amidst the frenzied clumping of wooden clogs.

Laying eyes on the city for the first time, Slainie was

awestruck by the tall brick shops in front of her, all connected in one long row. She darted between merchants and patrons as they bartered. She halted next to carts brimming with goods, only to race off again in an instant. Vincent and Jacques ran up stone walls and chased stray dogs. It was Saturday, and the city was noisy with Walloons breaking from work. Slainie waved to a man yelling, "Oysters! Today's fresh oysters!" and she hugged a chocolatier standing outside of her shop, passing out samples of bonbons.

Freeing herself from Mrs. Lafont's hand, Cecilia ran toward Slainie for a sample. Then, with chocolate smeared across her cheek, Cecilia jumped to a cart that caught her eye. She reached for a porcelain trinket box.

"I want one!"

Slainie grabbed her arm before she could snatch the small box with its hinged lid—and probably break it.

"I want that one, the one with strawberries on it." As Slainie pulled her sister away, Cecilia strained to reach the cart's display shelf.

"No, Cilia. Stop."

"Yes, Lainie." Cecilia threw herself on the ground.

Their parents were now uncomfortably far away, pushed along at the pace of the crowds. Kneeling next to her sister, Slainie spoke slowly and clearly, the way her mother often did. "Cilia. You know I have no money, and Papa and Mother are going on without us."

With a sudden widening of her eyes, Cecilia stopped wailing and allowed herself to be pulled off the ground. When they caught up to their family, Mrs. Lafont was complaining about the stench of garlic emanating from food carts and the many Belgians hawking their wares in Flemish instead of the regional French that the Lafonts spoke. Slainie's father put his arm around his wife. "French in the parlor. Flemish in the kitchen," he jested, and Mrs. Lafont took his hand.

Slainie surged ahead until she saw the canal. There, she stopped. Leaning against the side of the bridge, she watched the water splashing below. Moisture on the breeze spritzed her cheeks and the clean earthiness of the shores filled her nose. The merchants in their little boats waved up at her as the current pulled them along.

From the canal, the Lafonts walked down a road lined with candles in hanging glass jars. They turned on a brick path where four stone steps led to the house. Slainie tried to see past the panel of Brussels lace hanging down over the door's window. When the door opened, Mr. and Mrs. Lafont were greeted with several long handshakes. Slainie was immediately sent into a guest bedroom to play with all of the other children.

Slainie had felt odd the first time she went into that room. She had never been shut up with strange children before. But that visit made the move to America feel real for the first time. It was more than talk between her parents now. There, while the adults planned their voyage, the children who would later become settlement neighbors first met each other.

Over the coming weeks, Slainie talked much with Marie, whose parents were hosting the meetings. Marie was six also. Slainie told Marie that America was going to be beautiful, because the land was so wild. Marie thought it was going to be lonely, because they wouldn't know anyone. When they played, some of the children pretended to be lost at sea, throwing quilts in the air like giant waves and diving underneath. Marie pretended to be a big bear and chased the littlest ones up the sturdy oak bedposts. She grabbed at them as they hollered. Eventually, Slainie became so excited for these playdates she couldn't sleep the night before.

Sunbeams broke into the shadowy forest around Slanie, bringing her wandering mind into focus. She could see the side of Marie's Wisconsin home where the trail cut something like an arched doorway through the trees. This house was wooden instead of brick, but it was spacious and inviting—cozy, even—much like her city house had been.

When Slainie stepped out of the woods, Mrs. Martin stood barefoot in her yard, hanging wet clothes on a line. "*Bon après-midi*. Good afternoon."

Slainie approached. "Bonjour, *Madame*. Hello."

"Come. Come into the shade. Do you see the leaves? They are starting to turn dark red and bright yellow as though autumn will come, but the sun is still trying to make things grow."

Mrs. Martin set an armful of clothes in a giant basket and led Slainie to the front of the house. "You can go in and sit at the table. Marie's just finishing her lesson."

At the kitchen table, Marie sat with a broad-shouldered woman. Slainie stepped closer and immediately recognized the black cloak.

"*Coucou*! Hi! Hi!" said Marie, when she saw Slainie. "Mademoiselle Brise, can Slainie sit with us?"

Adele gently nodded. Slainie slunk into a chair next to them. *Why is this woman here? Doesn't she ever go home?* Slainie eyed the wood grains in the tabletop. Every once in a while Adele turned to her, but she never found the courage to look up. She felt humiliated. *Should I apologize for this morning? Does she think I'm horrible like my mother?* Then slowly, her feelings turned to curiosity. *Does that thing hurt? Would one call it an eye now? A wound? Just a hole? How does Marie keep from staring at it this whole time? I am not going to look at her at all. That's what I will do.*

Adele spoke in French. She breathed her words softly to Marie like she was revealing an important secret. She kept using the word "sacraments," and she asked Marie to tell her what sacraments she could remember from their lessons. Marie said, "Baptism, anointing of ill persons, confirmation, holy orders, penance, and—I don't remember. I'm sorry. My head is full of unfamiliar terms."

Adele smiled. "Marriage and the Eucharist. Remember? Repeat after me. These words are from our Lord: 'He that eateth my flesh and drinketh my blood shall obtain everlasting life.'"

Marie repeated the words. "I remember now."

With an encouraging tone, Adele took Marie's hands in hers. "In a few months, after completing your lessons, we will travel to Bay Settlement for your first confession. After this, you may eat Jesus' body and blood."

Slainie's head shot up. *A man's body? What is all this? Maybe this woman is insane after all.* She looked to see if Marie was thinking the same thing.

Marie suddenly sat tall in her chair. A grin replaced her serious expression. "Please tell Slainie about Our Lady."

Shaking her head, Adele turned to Slainie. "No. No. I must go now, but *you* may come with me someday . . . to the spot where I saw her."

Adele walked to the door, gently touched the cross on the wall, and then left.

Slainie lunged across the table and grabbed Marie's arm. "That woman came to my house just this morning! My mother was truly upset. She would not let her in. How awful is her face. How can you stand it?"

"Oh, she really is fine. I was only scared of her at first."

"*My* mother? She would never let me study with Adele." Slainie shook her head. "Almost every day she tells me I need to get better at sewing. Learning anything else is a waste of time, except maybe caring for the sick."

"Really? Like a doctor's apprentice? Then why does she make you sew all the time?"

"I don't know. I don't even like it."

Marie stood up. "Come to the porch with me."

Slainie stumbled to catch up. "How often does Adele come? Do you feed her? Does she ask for anything?"

"She comes every few days. She usually goes out to the garden. Sometimes, she kneads dough, right at the table with me. My mother says she walks through the woods for days at a time, going from house to house."

Marie grabbed her dolls off of a shelf in the living room.

"Where does she go then?"

Marie shrugged. "I think she has a family here in the settlement. Maybe she stays with them."

The chubby-cheeked head of Marie's china doll was white and shiny with painted black hair. Her other doll was a bisque. It had a ceramic head. She had carried it in her hands the entire way to Wisconsin. Slainie was there when Marie's grandfather had given it to her. It was one piece of Belgium that her friend couldn't leave behind.

The doll reminded Slainie of her sister, Cecilia. When she was only four, Cecilia had tried to pay for Slainie's ticket to Germany to see Marie's grandfather. Working as a painter, he brushed the tiny faces on the heads of bisque dolls. When the faces were done, he sent the heads to France where they were put together with fabric bodies and dressed like royalty. Marie bragged once that rich women all over the world were ordering the French dolls and giving them to their tailors. The *grande dames*, great women, would have perfect copies of the doll's clothing made for themselves.

A trip to Germany would have been long, almost seven days

by wagon and train. How Slainie had wished to see the beautiful dolls being made there, but Mrs. Lafont said no. They didn't have the money for such a trip.

"You can buy your own train ticket," Cecilia had said.

"I don't have any money."

Cecilia presented her coins to Slainie. "Then I will pay. I have two francs. You can use them."

Slainie patted her sister's head. "The money you have is only enough to buy a *galette*, Cilia. Only one small cookie."

"Not so. Just take it." Cecilia slapped the silver coins into Slainie's hand.

"It's not enough," Slainie insisted.

"But I want a dolly in Thuria too," Cecilia whined, struggling with the pronunciation of Thuringia.

Slainie smiled. "Yes, fine, *maybe* what you have is enough."

"It is. I am certain." Cecilia stomped off. "I'll ask Mama."

Slainie never did see the doll factory. Now, secluded in the woods, she was only glad to have such pretty dolls to play with. Coming to life out on Marie's porch, Slainie's china doll asked the bisque doll about her attire.

"Today? These are straight from my tailor this morning!" Marie held her chin high. She always thought it funny to describe the outfit using her grandfather's exact words. "My gown is taffeta, made with only the softest silk. *Oui*, yes, and it's trimmed with lace imported from the far, Far East. As far as you can go, I'm sure."

She placed the doll on its stand and smoothed its dress down to the floor.

"Would you be so generous as to allow me to touch your dress, *Madame*? Just a slight touch?" Lying on its face, Slainie's doll was practically groveling.

"Yes, but only after washing your hands first."

Smiling, Slainie took the small, frozen hand of the china doll with the thumb sticking out and clumsily patted the bottom of the dress on Marie's doll.

"Enough!" said Marie. "Now, I will allow you to borrow this priceless necklace."

The doll's necklace glimmered with alternating fake rubies and crystals. Of course, the rich women who owned the dolls would have necklaces with real gems made for themselves. Marie had several accessories for her doll. She told Slainie that every time her grandfather visited Namur he brought her another piece. She managed to fit a few of these gifts in her coat pockets to bring overseas—a tiny beaded bag, some hair combs and a miniature perfume bottle with real perfume inside. Sometimes the two girls would smell the perfume, but they would never use it.

Slainie gasped dramatically. "I dropped the necklace."

"I will never *ever* forgive you! My servant will see you to the door. You are never *ever* to come calling at my palace again!"

Marie's doll slumped to the floor. Marie moved the doll's little booted feet, as if she were kicking a fit. Laughing, the girls leaned into each other.

After dinner, Marie and her older brother walked Slainie home. A single candle's flame glowed softly in her cabin's back window, and a lantern flickered by the wood pile. Slainie's father leaned against the house, rubbing his tired eyes. After spotting her, he pretended to stack wood on the pile. His presence there didn't surprise Slainie. He always did this when she was out past dark, to calm his worries. Though it made her feel special, her gut ached, a feeling she habitually ignored. *Is it what happened to Cecilia that makes Papa so concerned for me, and so often?*

The children walked close enough to recognize Mr. Lafont smiling warm-heartedly. Marie hugged Slainie. "*Bonsoir.* Goodnight." As Mr. Lafont waved, he thanked them for bringing Slainie home. Then, he took Slainie's hand, and they went inside.

CHAPTER FOUR

Across Sea

1853 / 18 years before the fire

THE LAFONTS NEVER spoke about their immigration experiences—nothing mentioned of the discarded possessions, faring the seas, or the search for land to settle. Slainie dared not speak about leaving Belgium, because of the tragedy that followed. Immigrating and tragedy were one in Slainie's mind. The first had caused the latter.

In the months leading to their departure, Slainie felt a constant anticipation, like a snake looping around in her stomach. She often imagined the moment her parents would pick a parcel of American land: the family laughing together and the children locking arms and frolicking in high green grasses. This daydream marked the end of their arduous travels and the beginning of a promising new life. Despite her dreaming, that pent-up energy never flowed into joyous relief as Slainie had imagined it would. Nothing happened as anyone expected, and the Lafonts were scarred by what they lost when they came to America. A woman of extremes, no one hardened as much as Mrs. Lafont.

During the move, Cecilia struggled the most, even if she was as excited as everyone else. She could never sit still. She incessantly demanded Slainie hug her, kiss her, carry her, or "play something" with her. Every day after playing outside, she would burst into their hut and ask Mrs. Lafont if today was a "planning day," referring to the trips they took to Marie's city house in Namur.

One night at Marie's, Cecilia was jumping uncontrollably on the bed. "Look at me. Look at me. I'm the tallest bear! I AM the tallest!" She bellowed, landing so hard she knocked other children off the bed. Hiding underneath, Slainie pushed against the buckling planks above her head. Suddenly, at floor level, she spotted the door open, followed by the *clomp* of clogs.

"Settle down! All of you!" Slainie's mother ordered. "You have been disrupting us in the other room." Her voice cracked as she tried to yell over the noise. Even as Cecilia continued bouncing, Mrs. Lafont never returned to reprimand her. Slainie's mother had a soft spot for her middle daughter. Everyone did. The four-year-old charmed perfect strangers in the street.

Mrs. Allard must have seen something promising in Cecilia. Around that time, Cecilia had taught herself how to tie bows. She tied pieces of twine, thread, and rags to the legs of the table and the chairs in their hut, and even to Mr. Lafont's tools. They were so clumsily tied and so adorable that their mother never removed them. Instead, she decided to teach Cecilia to sew. Slainie had been sitting by the campfire near their hut when she overheard them. Curious, she peered inside through a tiny hole where the logs didn't sit level with one another.

Mrs. Lafont's voice sounded sweet and smooth like taffy. "Now, look closely. I can show you again."

Illuminated by a small lantern, Cecilia sat in her mother's lap. Mrs. Lafont held a needle and a bit of cloth in front of them.

"Take the needle here. Wait—just put your fingers on mine, and we will push the needle through. Then my other hand—you see it?—my other hand will grab the needle from below, rotate it, and push it back up."

Their mother pushed the needle in, and on the way out, said, "Now, you grab the needle there and pull the thread out. Slowly, now. Go slowly or the thread will bunch."

Slainie slunk around to the door of the hut.

"See, I knew you could," Mrs. Lafont exclaimed. "I'm going to tell your papa we have the smartest four-year-old in the world."

As she crawled unnoticed into her bed, Slainie couldn't help wishing there was something special about herself that their mother would brag about.

That night at Marie's house, even after Mrs. Lafont charged into the guest room to yell at the children, Cecilia kept pouncing and rolling like a feral cat on the bed. Annoyed, Slainie was about to wriggle out from beneath the bed and wag her finger in Cecilia's face, when the little one finally tired herself and lay down. Her brown hair cascaded over the mattress edge. Slainie scooched toward the swaying strands and gently pulled out the snarls. In her own way, Cecilia was dealing with the same uncertainty Slainie felt. Life was about to change in big ways. Jumping dangerously on a bed and other explosions of energy were Cecilia's way of coping with her anticipation.

A few months later, the Lafont family travelled to the port city of Antwerp. Slainie sat on a chest next to the Scheldt River, which would carry them out to sea. All around her, people were hugging and crying. Crates and suitcases lay strewn up and down the berth. A crew of sturdy longshoremen came down the dock, rolled up their blue sleeves, and set to loading the ship. Maneuvering through the crowd, they hefted luggage in each hand up the gangplank. When the dock was cleared, a long line of Belgians and Dutchmen boarded the *Quinnebaug* to sail to New York.

Slainie marked the moment she stepped on board as the moment she became an immigrant. She felt older as she breathed the salty air. Her family found their assigned bunks two levels below deck, where they sat in silence, swaying gently with the tide.

Cecilia squirmed on Slainie's lap trying to find a comfortable position. "This is an adventure."

Slainie bounced her knees, waiting for the ship to embark. "If you think so, maybe."

"Yes, Cilia." Mrs. Lafont frowned at Slainie. "It *is* an adventure. One that will never end."

On the schooner, Slainie quickly learned the only place to venture was the edge of one's bunk. Passengers rarely left their cabins, which soon smelled of sweat and unwashed bodies. The floors were filthy, and the children and their families had to clean everything themselves. The only place a person could breathe fresh air was up on deck in the one sequestered area for passengers. By sunrise each day, this small area teemed with people. Only the smallest of children could wedge in between the weary travelers for a glimpse of sky.

Of course, Cecilia discovered a covert exit from the confined passengers' deck. She told Slainie and Marie, who then slipped under the ropes after her. They hid behind barrels and rigging equipment to spy on sailors repairing torn sails or painting rotted boards. Soon, other children followed them. When the seas were calm, dozens of them gathered silently at the foot of one particular sailor. They watched as he stared into the small opening of a glass bottle. Piece by piece, steadily and gently, he placed bits of rope and whittled wood inside. Over several weeks, a tiny ship began to take form. The sailor didn't seem to mind the audience, unless he spotted the man in the high-ridged cap. This was the captain, as the golden embroidered anchor on his cap announced.

When storms arose, the winds blew giant waves across the deck, sending everyone to their cabins. One night, a harsh *snap* woke Slainie. Later, she learned the storm had broken a mast in half. Below decks, the violent pitching and rolling of the ship threatened passengers with flying dishes and chests full of clothes. Mr. and Mrs. Lafont shoved Slainie and her siblings under their bunks for protection.

The third week aboard, Slainie lost all joy for this nautical adventure. She became seasick and spent the rest of the voyage in her sticky, hot bunk. She shared the bed with her brother Jacques, and they turned and thrashed to find a comfortable position at their opposite ends. Some nights, she found comfort in a melodic dulcimer feebly strummed by one of the other Belgians. Mr. Lafont often reclined in his bunk with Cecilia's head in his lap. The little one had also taken ill.

Days passed as Slainie slipped in and out of sleep. One day, she heard a man's voice yelling, "Line up. Health check! Everyone line up." She thought the unkindly voice a dream until it grew so close and so loud it woke her. Swaying only slightly, the ship was no longer surging forward. Struggling to sit, Slainie cowered in the corner of her bed against the wall. Fellow passengers rose from their cots and lined up where the man with a clipboard had pointed.

Nearby, Mr. Lafont stood, but Cecilia wouldn't budge. Slainie's mother slapped her hand several times. Finally, she splashed Cecilia's face with a cup of water, and Mr. Lafont put his hands under her armpits, lifting her to stand. She moaned and whined, but stayed on her feet by leaning on others. Slainie let her feet fall to the floor, weightless under her. Wobbling as she tried to stand, they gave out, so she sat and listened to the man with the clipboard command the weary passengers on deck. Above them, the passengers shuffled past him. "Open your mouth. Stick out your tongue. Let me see your eyes. Look up. Next. Open your mouth. Stick out your tongue . . ."

Mrs. Lafont tugged Slainie's arm. "It's only a health check."

Slainie joined the line. The Collector of Customs needed to scan each passenger for fevers, sweating, rashes and other signs of illness. Only if the ship was free of any serious contagion would he permit them to dock.

Jacques brushed up against her back. "I heard a ship from Ireland was kept at bay for three weeks." He stepped back a few inches. "They waited until all fevers broke before anyone could put a toe on land. We may be held here for some time."

With a growing worry, Slainie listened to all of the coughing, sniffling and grunting around her. Jacques might be right.

CHAPTER FIVE

Across Land

1853 / 18 years before the fire

AFTER SIX WEEKS at sea, Slainie ached to walk on stable ground. There was only one thing stopping her. *Please stop coughing, everyone. Stop sounding so sick.* She inched forward with each "Next!" until she stepped out of her cabin. Ascending the stairs, she emerged into sunshine—and right under the uniformed man's nose. A naval officer stood next to him, both peering at Slainie. She tried to stand more firmly, straight and alert. Instead, she squinted and winced at the sun. Though she felt faint, they couldn't tell. "Next!" the uniformed man shouted, and Slainie shuffled back below deck as quickly as she could.

Now, Slainie waited on her bunk, again swaying anxiously with the tide. The ship creaked into motion. *We must be going toward the docks.* Slainie didn't know what to expect. When it was her family's turn to disembark, she stood at the top of the berth that slanted down to a dock. *This is New York City.*

Rectangular slips were lined up before her like piano keys—water, dock, water, dock—with massive ships nestled in some of them. Slainie peered through miles of ropes and pulleys. Each slip had a number. Hers was number *39 Burling*. Next to the wooden number sign, there was another sign with arrows carved into it. Each arrow pointed to a nearby street. Market Street. Watts Street. Canal Street. Slainie glanced back across the sea before descending the berth. The foggy, flat horizon was dotted with patches of land and assorted ships whose colorful flags waved at the top of their masts, designating their homelands through the haze.

On the wharf, men dragged luggage off of the ship, dropping it amidst the frantically bustling crowd. Many children draped themselves on the ground, some crying. Several mothers offered foreign coins to a street vendor for a decent meal, too frazzled to remember they needed to exchange their currency first. Tall office buildings and tenements lined the streets. The spires and domes of several churches rose up from behind them.

Down the street, six black horses nickered as they hauled a wagon packed with giant barrels. Spotting a pudgy man with a push cart, Slainie leapt in his direction. Her stomach ached with hunger, and his cart was piled high with triangular puffed pastries. Coming nearer, she heard the man holler, "Appelflap." They smelled like cinnamon and warm apples, but before she could ask for one, Mr. Lafont grabbed her hand and started dragging her from office to office.

"What are we doing, Papa?"

Mr. Lafont stepped through a doorway, looked around and stepped out. "I bought combination tickets. They're supposed to take us overseas and then across land. But we need to locate an agent for Strauss Shipping Company. He'll have our accommodations ready."

Every agent he spoke to said they hadn't heard of Strauss. He couldn't find anyone who would honor his tickets. In office after office, merchants turned their backs to him, until one finally muttered, "Go ask your captain." Slainie trailed her father until he found the man from the *Quinnebaug* with the anchor on his cap.

"What do you mean there is no wagon?" her father asked.

"I'm sorry, sir," the captain said, as he tied some rope to a piling. "You'll have to pay again for land transport to wherever it is you plan to go."

"Look here. Look at this." Mr. Lafont held up his ticket, but the captain kept working.

"I know what it says, sir. I have seen these papers before. They are a fake . . . a common swindle."

Mr. Lafont stomped down the berth to where Mrs. Lafont waited. He didn't tell her that he had to pay again for all the necessities of traveling across the country. With what little money and possessions they had, Slainie worried they didn't have the money for new tickets. The next day, though, Mr. Lafont had secured a spot for them on a wagon train going north to the Erie Canal.

As the wagon bounced along, Cecilia coughed harshly. She was still sick. She had stopped eating on the ship and lie clutching her chest. She hadn't the energy to lift her own head, and her lips dried up and cracked, even though Mrs. Lafont gave her sips of water every few minutes. Slainie wanted to hold Cecilia's hand or caress her forehead. She wanted to do something to stop her sister's moaning. Yet, with baby Modette on her lap, she couldn't do much but hope they would find help for Cecilia at the next town.

Resting was impossible, though Slainie had made a pile of clothing and blankets for her and the baby to lie on. Suitcases and boxes towered and wobbled next to them. For days they would ascend to highlands. Then the wagon would slant down toward some valley floor. Once or twice, Slainie feared the wagon would flip end over front. Slainie could barely breathe in the August heat, and any breeze was blocked by Mr. Lafont and the boys sitting in the driver's bench. Modette also radiated heat in that way babies do. Slainie remained miserable until her father rolled up the sides of the canvas cover. Of course, then Mrs. Lafont feared the dust and dirt would hinder Cecilia's breathing, so the cover had to be lowered again. Once in a while, Slainie would startle to Modette's tiny hand on her face and be happy that she had fallen asleep for a short time.

When it rained, the wagons were on a trail through the forest. The children jumped out to wash themselves in the downpour. Marie meandered through the needled trees collecting wet pine cones in her smock with the other girls. She handed one to Slainie, who had to stay in the wagon with her sisters. Slainie longed to feel the freshness of rain on her dirty skin.

On the prairie, it rained again. The girls lifted their skirts to run in the green and yellow grasses. Slainie giggled at the boys wrestling and plucking handfuls of wild rye and mud to throw at each other. She thrust her arms out from under the wagon cover and craned her head to catch the cool rain on her tongue.

In the misty morning hours, Slainie's family counted hawks, ducks and songbirds for points. When an elk crossed them on the trail, Mr. Lafont joked that it counted for the most points and that he had won the game for seeing it first. Then he gave all his points to Cecilia, who could only acknowledge his gift by nodding. Slainie hoped they wouldn't see any black bears.

After riding north through New York, the Lafonts entered Canada. They travelled west until they reached the Great Lakes. Then, a steamboat took them across Lake Michigan. The lake appeared to be another never-ending ocean. Slainie feared she would be stuck seasick on it for weeks, but a day later, the boat docked at a place called Milwaukee.

Everywhere they went, Slainie's family enjoyed learning the Indian meaning behind a location's name. Milwaukee meant "pleasant land," and Slainie agreed with the Algonquin Indians in naming it thus. Slainie looked out across the earth. It was flat, easier to traverse. Two gentle rivers flowing through calm land.

From Milwaukee, the wagons rode to Sheboygan, a name that meant "passage between the lakes." In this passage, hundreds of Indians camped in colorful wigwams along the bluffs. Fear must have shone on Slainie's face as they rode past the wigwams, because Mr. Lafont suddenly said, "They're just here to trade their pelts. Heard it around the fire last night. They come for the tobacco, the whiskey and other things the Europeans make."

Slainie stared at the dark-haired men resting with their ponies in front of the general store. White settlers ate with them on the porches of their log homes. She gaped at the shirtless Indian women, using only their thick hair to cover themselves.

Mr. Lafont relaxed the oxen's reins and leaned back toward Slainie. "Bet they'll be gone tomorrow and won't come back for months."

Slainie begged her parents to stay there in Sheboygan. She wanted to stop moving, but her parents thought better land lay further north. The Lafont family followed the wagon train until they reached Kaukauna, or "the place of the pike."

Vincent pointed toward dozens of the yellow-speckled fish hanging on lines between cabins. "Look at them, Papa."

Jacques noticed some laid across logs to dry in the sun. "They are like monsters."

Some of the silvery giants stretched only a foot and a half, but others must have been four, even five feet long. The odor of the cleaning house, where the guts and scales were removed, soured the air as Slainie rode by. But, to her, it signaled that life was good in Kaukauna, because food was plentiful. She wanted to cut down some trees and build a lean-to that very day.

An American family from Connecticut welcomed the Lafonts

for the night. No doubt they were worried about Cecilia. Slainie surveyed the garden where dozens of yellow squash looked ready to burst. Giant tomatoes hung from bushes, so ripe and swollen some had simply slipped off their branches and splattered on the ground. The house was furnished with ornate chairs and paintings. It had many rooms and wide hallways, wide enough for small decorative tables to line the walls. Behind the house stood a horse stable, a chicken coop, an outhouse, goats, and a sheep shelter, where the Lafonts spent the night since the Americans were leery about the possible contagion of Cecilia's illness. No matter where they slept, Slainie wanted to stay there forever and never ride in that wagon again.

In the morning, Slainie and her siblings gathered their bedding from the hay-covered floor where they had slept. They packed up the wagon to start north on the trail again. Mr. and Mrs. Lafont trudged from cabin to cabin looking for a doctor who would see Cecilia before they left. The other Belgians they were traveling with agreed to wait for them. Several hours went by, and Modette whimpered and clawed at Slainie, who grew frustrated and tired of babysitting.

Finally, her parents appeared a little way off, and Slainie ran to them, leaving Modette in the grass.

"Are we staying?" she called out. "Can we stay?"

"Not certain yet," said her father.

Slainie looked at her mother. "Please, Maman."

Her mother lifted up the baby. "Go back to the wagon."

Mr. Lafont finally spoke, placing his hand on Slainie's head. "Children, we've made the acquaintance of a pleasant couple. They've called us to their parlor for tea, so . . . we'll see."

It was a woman with braids to her waist and a man with a curving mustache. They met the Lafonts on the path near their cabin. Slainie and her brothers wandered into the cornfield.

Making circles in the dirt with a piece of corn, Slainie waited in the shade of the stalks. A short while later, Mr. Lafont called the children. They could stay until Cecilia grew strong enough to continue north. They could stay in the pleasant couple's shed, but first it needed to be cleaned out. Mr. Lafont told the other Belgians in the wagon train, and the group continued north without them.

Inside the shed, picks and rakes lined the walls. Stacks of wooden crates rose to the ceiling. Vincent, Slainie's oldest brother, had loaded his arms with five or six crates, piled so high he couldn't see where he was going. He stumbled and caught himself on a small table, sending a bucket of oil and tins clattering to the floor. Slainie's mother quickly tugged her away from the mess. Waiting outside, they watched Mr. Lafont and the mustached man dump bucket after bucket of water across the floor. Vincent finally asked the woman with the braids what the fuss was about.

"I make soft soap for the settlement," she said. She pointed to a kettle on the ground near the fire pit. "I store animal fat and lye in the shed. That keeps children and animals from getting into trouble with it."

"How does it work?" Vincent asked, but he ran off to play before she answered.

"You'll probably need to make it, too," she said to Slainie. "The important thing is to stay away from the lye, at least until you know how it works. That's the poison your brother spilled on the floor. Tonight, you must sleep in the wagon. The breeze should clear the lye out by tomorrow."

That night, Mrs. Lafont slept under the wagon canopy with Cecilia and Modette. The rest of the Lafonts slept on makeshift beds of hay on the ground beside the wagon. As Slainie lay under the stars, she wondered what would come next. *Will we end up staying here? Will we grow gardens as beautiful as those I saw today?*

Or will we leave and wander again from town to town? Slainie wanted Cecilia to get better, but she also wanted to stay—and she knew she couldn't have both.

CHAPTER SIX

Cecilia

1853 / 18 years before the fire

BECAUSE CECILIA WASN'T allowed to leave the shed, Slainie rarely saw her during the following weeks. When she tried to visit, their mother narrowed her eyes and whispered "get" from behind the rag tied over her mouth. Slainie sat in the grass trying to catch glimpses of her sister when Mrs. Lafont emerged from the shed, but every time her mother left, she immediately shut the door and scrubbed her hands up to her elbows under the water pump.

Slainie tired of getting lost in the maze of corn rows all by herself. She wanted to bring Cecilia out to run in the fields. She picked flowers and found interesting stones, arranging them in a basket for their mother to place next to Cecilia's bed.

On the afternoon of their fourth day in Kaukauna, an elderly man arrived at the house. His long black coat reached all the way to his knees and tangled him up when he tried to dismount his horse. Slainie sat with Modette and watched from their spot in the grass. His heavy-looking bag clinked and sloshed as he walked to the door.

Later in the day, Slainie peeked in at her sister and saw the doctor still there. She pried the door open a bit, though she was afraid the man's dark eyes would peer out from under his bushy brows to scold her at any moment. He put drops of brown liquid in Cecilia's mouth, and every few minutes he would lean over and put his ear to her chest. When Cecilia flinched in her sleep, Slainie thought his long white beard must have tickled her face. Then the doctor sat in a chair and ran his fingers over his head of wispy hair.

"Mr. and Mrs. Lafont, it is consumption." His mouth moved under a strip of gauze tied behind his head. "Surely you knew that already."

Slainie stared at the doctor, confused, waiting for him to say more. Then, his face softened. "Apologies, poor child. This must be terribly frightening for you. I have given your sister a tincture of la-DUH-nuhm. It's a pleasant mixture for her, made mostly of honey. She's probably dreaming of candy treats now."

"Thank you, doctor." Mr. Lafont approached the bed and smoothed Cecilia's hair. "She's only four and . . ."

"I know. I know. Very well." The doctor stood and slid his arms into his coat. "She needs rest. Give this to her. The opium in this laudanum will help her sleep." He handed Mr. Lafont a small, amber-colored bottle. "It should soothe her stomach and loosen her chest so she can breathe more effectively. Then she should get fresh air, not near any water. No moisture should enter her lungs. I will come back with another bottle for you in a few weeks. It's best to keep everyone but her mother out of this room."

The next morning, Slainie came to the cabin and saw her hostess leaning against the wall, fiddling with her long braids. Startled by Slainie, her eyes shot up, and she said, "Go in there, little one." Slainie took a deep breath as she entered the shed and found she couldn't let it out. For days, she had longed to see her sister, but it wasn't her sister who she saw now.

Near the bed, her mother knelt crying. The blankets had been pulled over Cecilia's head. Her slender arm hung limp off the bedside. Slainie turned and stumbled back through the door. Her thoughts came frantically, and she fell against the shed wall. Pressing her cheek hard on a log, she tried to make sense of what was happening. *I don't understand. The doctor was just here. He fixed her. She's just too tired. They need to wake her. Throw water on her face. She's not dead. Rouse her! Just rouse her and you'll see!*

Then Slainie was weeping alone in the grass. Between sobs, she could hear her mother mumble angrily from the shed. Who could she go to? The woman with the braids who was still out in the yard? She wanted to get up, but her legs wouldn't respond. She just lay there sloppy with tears, drifting in and out of consciousness.

It must have been hours later that Slainie heard her father's boots stomp on the shed floor. Then more weeping, while Vincent and Jacques whispered outside. When her brothers tried to see Cecilia, Mrs. Lafont told them to go away. The woman with the braids suggested that they go in the house, and they left.

Slainie must have been in the grass with ants crawling around her all day, because when her father scooped her up, he took her straight to bed. As she lay next to her mother, she began to cry again. Mrs. Lafont just stared past her.

From his spot on the floor, Mr. Lafont raised an arm to touch Slainie. "Shh, shh. We're okay."

"What are we doing now?" Jacques whispered.

Silence filled the shed, heavy like the motionless dark all around them.

"I mean, where does Cecilia go now?"

Rolling to face Jacques, Mr. Lafont spoke with a voice that barely escaped his throat. "We have to wait a few days. A priest has been sent for, but he is some ways up north."

Suddenly, Mrs. Lafont sat up. "Hush. Go to sleep."
They all quieted.

A few days later, a young priest arrived in dusty black robes.
Before approaching the house, he paused to remove his wide-
brimmed hat and set it gently on his saddle. Slainie's parents came
outside. She heard them in disagreement with the priest on the
porch. He wanted Cecilia brought to another town to be buried
in "consecrated ground," which he explained was ground blessed
for burials.

Mrs. Lafont raised her hands to stop all the talking. "Sir, I
know what consecrated ground is. It's unnecessary. We will do
this right here. She is gone now, and she needs burying."

That afternoon, Slainie's brothers dug a hole in the ground on
the edge of the forest. Into the hole, they lowered her sister, so still
and small, swaddled like a baby in a red quilt. The priest, Father
Daems, spoke of the innocence and simplicity of children, declar-
ing that Cecilia went straight to heaven. He spoke about God's
love for children. Slainie didn't see love in Cecilia's death. She
looked to her mother for a sign that everything was going to be
all right, needing only a glance in her direction, an instant of ten-
derness. It never came. As she buried her child, Mrs. Lafont's face
remained twisted in anger and grief. She just went cold. Slainie
hugged Modette close to hide that she was crying.

For a long time, Slainie couldn't move from the grave. Flashes
of Cecilia flooded her mind—her soft brown hair, her gaunt face
in the wagon, and the last smile Slainie could remember, on the
ship when they found some bits of rope and began tying them
to everything. It had been Cecilia's idea to sit at the sailor's feet
while he made his ship-in-a-bottle. Slainie would have been con-
tent staying behind the barrels twenty feet away.

That evening, when they were eating supper, Father Daems

sat in the grass with Slainie and her siblings. He told them they were lucky to have such kind friends in Kaukauna. "Your sister died comfortably," he said and lowered his eyes. The boys glanced up for a moment, just to acknowledge he had spoken. Slainie wasn't eating, she was thinking. She was determined to stay in Kaukauna now. *We can't leave Cecilia here alone. We must stay. And there are farms and homes here, too.* Slainie figured they could clear some more trees and make their home next to the kind people who had taken them in. Next to Cecilia's grave.

Slainie thought Mr. Lafont had the same idea until Father Daems convinced him otherwise. The priest had told them stories about a town on Lake Michigan, a town full of Belgians. He was also from a French-speaking region of Belgium, and he knew exactly what these worn-out travelers needed—a few neighbors they could relate to.

Slainie spent three more days in Kaukauna, mostly in the yard with Modette. She watched the baby investigate rocks and grasses and tried to keep her from eating them. Many times, she followed the baby to the edge of the woods and carried her back to the cabin, only so she could try running away into the wild again.

Sometimes Slainie forgot about the tragedy. She would grab the baby as if to bring her closer to the shed, but halfway there remember that Cecilia wasn't inside. She would see Cecilia's arm and the quilt over her body. Once when Modette was sleepy, she lay down on Slainie's chest in the grass. Caressing the soft skin of the baby's cheeks, Slainie watched the clouds drift overhead. Traveling on the wind, the sound of women laughing as they gathered spices reached Slainie's ears. An hour must have passed, during which Modette's warmth spread to Slainie, igniting a surge of happiness. That is until the sudden realization that Cecilia was dead hit her. Again and again, she would forget. Again and again, with a wave of pain, she would remember.

The day they left Kaukauna, Slainie's mother placed a bouquet of wispy prairie grass and goldenrod flowers on the rock pile at Cecilia's grave. Then the Lafonts pushed on toward a town called Green Bay, where they would reunite with the rest of the Belgian immigrants. The cabin disappeared from sight, and the woman with the braids and the man with the mustache waved farewell until Slainie couldn't see them any longer.

Leaving broke her heart. Her stomach quivered, and she ached as though she had a fever. She fought to keep from crying and begging her father to go back. Instead, she whispered "goodbye," and curled around Modette trying to fall asleep. She never heard Mrs. Lafont speak of her dead child or the Kaukauna settlement again. All of her mother's stories and conversations were about the future, as if she had never lived before tomorrow.

When the wagon arrived at Bay Settlement, Slainie's stomach relaxed in relief to see a doctor's office, general store, blacksmith, and clusters of cabins, as if they were back in Kaukauna. Everywhere she looked, gleeful children bounded. Some played pick-up sticks in the dirt. Others had blindfolded a friend, spun him round, and then ran when he came chasing after them. She saw herself and Cecilia playing with these children. Then she remembered again that Cecilia was gone, and felt nothing when her father pushed the oxen onward, miles and miles away from anyone.

The wagon stopped when her father had located their fellow Belgians. A forest dense and dark surrounded them. The first few nights in those trees, Slainie slept on the ground, as did all of the new settlers. Gazing skyward, all she could see were tangled branches in the canopy above her. The settlers fashioned temporary lean-tos—three-walled structures, with an open side that faced away from prevailing winds. Slainie's elders decided on a name for their nascent settlement: *Aux Premier Belges*. The First Belgians.

Slainie worked alongside her siblings doing laundry and milking cows. They fed the sheep, pigs, chickens, and oxen. They foraged. Mostly, though, they spent their days digging up the roots and turning the soil where gardens and crops would one day grow.

Even with her two brothers and her baby sister to keep her company, Slainie was lonely. She missed her father, who was always working, just as he was in Belgium. Now, he was turning the Wisconsin trees into cabins, fences, kegs, benches, boxes, furniture, plows, and anything that needed to be built for normal life to begin. The settlers cut down trees for years, and still rows and rows of them stood huddled against the horizon. As the pine, hemlock, and spruce fell under Mr. Lafont's ax, he repeated time and again that "it's all troubles now, but the future is coming such as nothing we could have known in Belgium."

For five years, the Belgians lived entirely isolated from any other settlements. When Slainie was eleven, the men finally hacked trails through the woods for the wagons to ride on. They were rut-filled and often flooded, but they expanded the world for Slainie. She was finally able to bounce along on supply trips to Green Bay. Then the Lafonts built a second level on their cabin, which became the sleeping loft.

As the years passed, Slainie carried the pain of her sister's death in silence, because no one dared to speak about it. She missed Cecilia's irresistible personality. She missed the sound of her running throughout the house like a busy little squirrel. The years had whittled her memories down and what was left radiated her sister's joy. Cecilia had never hoarded her joy from anyone. She had filled every soul with joy like an orchestra performing Franz Joseph Hadyn.

Life as a settler, after the loss of her sister, had worn Slainie down. As a twelve-year-old, she felt small and insignificant among the trees of Northern Wisconsin. Nearly men, her brothers were occupied with work at home and throughout the settlements, building their own lives. Now seven years old, baby Modette was dutiful and seemed satisfied. Slainie, however, felt life like the Earth's rotation—achingly slow—with the sun rising on her hard labor and setting on her tired back. That is, until seven years after she immigrated, until the day Adele Brise knocked on the Lafonts' door.

CHAPTER SEVEN

Allard Family

1860 / 11 years before the fire

THERE WAS NO way to erase the wonder that meeting Adele had awakened in Slainie. Throughout autumn, as the smell of hearths and bonfires filled the forest, Slainie trekked to Marie's house as often as she could. She tried to visit on the days when she knew Marie would be receiving lessons from Adele. She listened to Adele for hours and hours, above the crackling of the wood burning stove.

As winter settled in, her curiosity intensified in the absence of Adele's lessons. Each day, after completing their work, Slainie and her siblings sat around their stove. The cabin was frigid. The wind blew through gaps in the logs, shooting little puffs of snow past them as if the indoors were outside. They took turns supplying logs for a fire they could never let die. Otherwise, one of them would have to trudge through snow to the neighbors for coals to start a new one. In the evening, Mr. Lafont returned with his rifle on his back and stories to keep them entertained all evening. If they were lucky, he'd also have a deer slung over his shoulders.

Slainie saw Adele only twice during the winter: once at Marie's and once on the sled trail. Adele was pushing against a snowdrift, fighting to keep her steps inside the footprints already packed deeply into the snow. A wool scarf was wrapped in layers about her head. Her tattered coat appeared useless against the cold.

As Slainie watched from the wagon bed, she pulled a fur-fringed hood tightly around her face. *I wonder if she recognizes me.* She almost jumped out to greet Adele, who turned her head to watch them pass without pausing her plodding progress. Strange how Adele could be out there in the snow with how cold it got in that wild country. No one wanted to go out in those storms, not even housebound children with nothing better to do. Yet Adele walked fifty miles to some of the homes where she was teaching.

One weekend, Marie's family came to supper. The children bundled themselves in wool long johns, jackets, scarves, and doubled-up socks. The most recent snowfall left thick, sticky blankets on the iced-over stream. It took time to clear the ice with branches, but soon the boys and girls, young and old, had cleared it together. The stream glistened welcomingly with a slippery flat surface. A few of the children used their clogs to dig tracks into a small hill along the bank. They slipped and sledded down onto the ice until their limbs froze.

As they played, Slainie prodded Marie for answers about Adele. "It's still odd to me to just walk up to a stranger's door like that."

Marie's teeth chattered audibly. "She has a m-m-m-ission. The Virgin Mary gave it to her when sh-sh-she was walking through Robinsonville."

"The who?" asked Slainie.

"You know, the Mother of J-j-jesus. A few months after

th-th-that, her father built a chapel near the spot."

"Like a church?"

"No. It's small, like a wayside chapel for t-t-travelers. Do you r-r-rem-m-member those in Belgium? They only held a couple people, and this one's no b-b-bigger than a wagon bed."

When spring came, Slainie couldn't suffer her curiosity any longer, and she decided to go to Robinsonville to see for herself. Because it was Saturday, delivery day, she was headed in the direction of the chapel anyway. She woke up earlier than usual for the long trek, found the clothes under her pillow, pulled the blanket over her head, and pulled her dress on underneath it. Dropping down from her loft quickly, like she did every morning, made her dress fall to her ankles before anyone could see. Vincent and Jacques were still asleep in their bunks, and Mr. Lafont had gone to work, but Mrs. Lafont was already shelling peas at the table with Modette.

Slainie tied some bread and dried meat in a cloth and dropped it in the sack of clothes she was delivering to the Allard family. She expected the Allards to invite her to stay for supper, and as long as she was back before dark, she knew her mother wouldn't say a thing.

"Don't forget to bring next week's mending home with you," Mrs. Lafont called out.

Slainie quickly carried her secret plan out the door. "Yes, Maman."

The morning cast an orange glow on everything, and all was quiet, except for a red-breasted robin at the top of a pine. It sang as if it had a rooster's job of waking the entire woods. Slainie spotted some squirrels dashing down branches and back up. Her eyes glimmered in the sunlight as she imagined seeing Adele again. Warm sun beams came through the trees, illuminating different spots on the ground. Some ancient roots wound down into the dirt. Chubby mushrooms were bejeweled in dew. A million ferns were unfurled. Her steps crackled a chorus atop needles and twigs.

When she had gone a mile, Slainie stepped out of the trees and glimpsed the Allard farm. There was the large garden, colorful with carrot tops, potatoes, leeks, herbs, and blooming berry bushes. Next to the garden stood the old cabin, the one the Allards built when they had just arrived. It was simple, like Slainie's house, except now it was a barn for the cows and oxen. Beside that sat the hen and hog pens. Behind those, a threshing house. The Allards lived in a larger, newer cabin, which had wood floors instead of dirt and separate rooms for girl and boy children. It even had curtains on the windows and an organ, which Slainie's friends were learning to play.

Slainie spotted the two eldest boys out in a field that stretched so far it curved with the earth. Looking as small as pigeons, they dug out one of a thousand naked tree stumps, breaking up its root so more crops could be planted. The project had started seven years earlier, when the Belgians had cleared their very first trees.

Slainie approached the house and Zoe, who was eighteen, ran from the barn to greet her. On her heels was Marguerite, who was thirteen, like Slainie. Their fifteen-year-old brother Joseph sprinted over with a fence post in his arms, and the youngest, Henri sauntered up with more bravado than the other three Allard boys combined.

"What has our *Petite Ourse,* Littlest Bear, brought us now?" Henri tossed a clump of dirt at her.

Slainie had met the Allards seven years ago at Marie's city house in Belgium. All of the children had bonded during the move to America, but none were as adored by Slainie as Henri.

Seeing him now, she remembered the evening they had spoken for the first time. They were in Marie's guest room in Namur, and Slainie's brothers had crept down the dark hallway to listen to the grownups in the parlor. When Marie's father came to check on the children, Vincent and Jacques dashed back inside the room.

Pretending he had been there the whole time, Vincent plopped down on the wide arm of the chaise Slainie was lounging in. Leaning near her face, he whispered, "It's going to be horrible for you in America. Little girls are eaten by wolves and bears there all the time."

Her head down, Slainie couldn't look at Vincent. "No. No, they aren't."

"Yes, they are, and there's no one to protect you, because no one lives there."

He grinned and put his forehead to hers. "Mother said so."

Forced to look into his fixed eyes, Slainie couldn't hide her fear. She squirmed away and sat on the floor, watching the other children play happily. *Bears don't eat little girls. I have never ever heard that . . . but maybe they do in America.*

Then she noticed four-year-old Henri Allard lying under the bed. He had crawled under to hide, because it was his turn to be the littlest bear in a game all of the children were playing.

Marie called out, "*Orson? Orson?* Bear cub? Where are you, *Tres Petit Ours?*" but he wasn't yowling for help like the other "bears" were. From her spot near the bed, Slainie heard what sounded like genuine whimpering. Looking under, she saw his head cradled in his arms. The others didn't notice when she slid under next to him.

She tapped his shoulder. "My mother says America is a good place. I believe her."

She may have been reassuring herself, but it seemed to help him. The two of them lay there, looking up at the wooden planks under the mattress. Cecilia began jumping on the bed above them, and they shielded themselves with their arms in case the planks snapped in their faces.

When it was time for bed, the children shuffled off to couches or piles of blankets on the floor. After rolling out from under the bed, Henri bent down to look at Slainie. "Next week, you can be the littlest bear with me again."

With a sack of mended clothing swung over her shoulder, Slainie could hardly believe that little Henri-under-the-bed was this brawny eleven-year-old that stood before her now in the new country. Brushing the dirty hair off his brow, he took the sack of clothes from Slainie and strolled toward his family's cabin.

Zoe pushed her hair back under her scarf. Slainie noticed strands of grass around her forehead and leaned in to pluck them off. A giant smile shone from under the dirt and freckles on Zoe's face. She put her arm up and around Slainie's neck.

"You're always going to be taller than I am," she said.

Marguerite breathed deeply and huffed it out. "Come, *les enfants*, children. We should not mill about when Mama has called us to supper."

Turning toward the house, she motioned with a dainty finger for them to follow. With the poise of a duchess, she lifted her dress and took tiny steps through the yard. Slainie didn't notice even one strand of Marguerite's hair out of place as the blond threads swayed back and forth at her waist.

As all of the children piled into the house, Slainie scanned the table for her favorite Belgian dish. There it was: *stoemp*—potatoes mashed with vegetables. Mrs. Allard mixed the potatoes with an unnecessary amount of milk fat, so it looked fluffy like whipping cream. Today, the fluff came with bits of onions, carrots, and chives.

Mrs. Allard took a kettle off the cast-iron stove that had tiny, painted flowers on it. "*Bon apres midi*, Slainie. Good afternoon. Sit. Sit. Did you yet see the puny lamb out in our barn?"

"No, *madame*, I've only just arrived."

"I wouldn't have believed it myself had I not been there. One of our dear ewes gave us three lambs last week. Highly irregular." Mrs. Allard set the kettle on the table.

Marguerite covered her mouth as she chewed. "The third is a disappointment."

Mrs. Allard nodded at Marguerite. "The children are on shifts to feed the poor baby. She is part of the family now."

"I hope by next week the imp will have grown enough that we don't need to run out to the barn every time the wind blows," Marguerite responded.

Joseph tore off a piece of bread. "Three lambs are worth more than two."

"Precisely," agreed Mrs. Allard. "Well, Slainie, don't be a timid lamb yourself. Please, fill your plate."

As Slainie reached for the ladle, the front door opened. Mr. Allard entered followed by a giant of a man. Pressed and collared, his jacket had shiny brass buttons up the front. With big steps, he clunked across the room, sat and rested his boots on the table's edge. Mr. Allard took a seat next to the man's feet and clasped his hands. Slainie and the Allard children spooned food into their mouths in silence.

"Mr. Lincoln is head of the race," the man said, ignoring the presence of anyone else in the room. "We in the east and you in the north, we all need to put our full support behind him, even if that means war. Tell me, Claude, when war comes, what would you pay to spare your boys from it?"

Mr. Allard straightened and looked long at Henri, Joseph, Jacques and Leon.

"You *could* buy replacements for them. It's something you'd
be able to afford. But, hear me now, you . . . want . . . this . . .
war." The man leaned close to Mr. Allard with a white-toothed
grin.

"Mr. Crane, forgive me, but I don't know where I stand on
war with the South."

Slainie listened, slowly savoring her potatoes like ice cream.
The man's heavy voice turned the children's ears, but they kept
their eyes on their forks.

"This is my offer: together, we'll break in the rest of your soil.
You give me 40 percent of the profit. I'll provide laborers and—"

"If I may," interrupted Mrs. Allard, "what kind of men are
these?"

"My men are of good stock. I assure you, there wouldn't be
any trouble."

"I still don't see what a war has to do with my fields," said
Mr. Allard.

Mr. Crane spooned himself a plate of *stoemp*, tasting it with
a dipped finger before he took a bite. "The demand for wheat will
blow sky-high. You've got the land, and I've got reapers and the
machines you need. There's no farmer in a hundred miles with the
kind of machinery you'll have."

"Machinery," mumbled Mr. Allard, relaxing into his chair.

"Now, let me make this clear. The Jayhawkers, those are the
Yanks in Kansas, they're mounting against the rebels down south.
Only small skirmishes here and there, but come time for Lincoln
to take the presidency, Missouri, Louisiana—hell, I heard half of
Virginia is going to leave the Union."

Zoe whispered, "What are Yanks?" No one answered.

"We would certainly not oppose any effort to release the
slaves down south," said Mr. Allard.

"Soldiers need to eat, and your wheat would be carried right to Union camps on those fancy new railways." Mr. Crane turned his whole body toward Slainie, Zoe, and Marguerite, who were sitting at the end of the table. "I see here three strong girls. Do you girls know how to mend clothes? Can you clean a wound?"

Mrs. Allard patted the air with her hands, then motioned toward the stairs. "*D'accord. D'accord.* Okay, enough. We needn't get ahead of ourselves."

The children left their plates half-full and went upstairs. The men's voices faded as Slainie followed Zoe and Marguerite to their room.

"Did any of that make sense to you?" asked Zoe.

Slainie and Marguerite shook their heads. Zoe pushed the curtain open, revealing a blue sky over the tops of trees. The familiar buzz of cicadas filled the room. Marguerite took out a small box from under her bed.

"What's in there?" Slainie asked.

"These are my Indian beads." Marguerite dumped some into her hand.

Slainie plucked out three beads. She admired the carvings in each blue and white shell as she cupped them in her hand. Most children Slainie knew had souvenirs from the Indians. The easiest to get were arrowheads. Children often found those in the woods. Some children had claw pendant necklaces, and her Papa was given a tobacco pipe carved from bone when an Indian guide coveted his leather suspenders.

"Where did you get those?" Slainie asked.

"I left New York with two bags of glass beads, the ones my pa bought me. On the trail, we came upon some good-natured Indians resting with their horses. They were leading a wagon train. My brothers tried to scare me with so many tales of the strangeness of them and stories of their battles, but I wasn't scared at all."

"You just went up to them?" Slainie rolled the beads between her fingers as she listened.

"*Ouais*, of course, and I traded just ten little glass beads for all these."

Slainie picked up two more beads. "They gave you a whole bag of their beads for just ten of your own?"

Marguerite nodded, trying to suppress a smile.

"Entirely unjust," declared Zoe. "It's not fair to trade with those poor, uneducated people. Not when they have no way to understand what the trade means."

"Come, Zo. They are more intelligent than you think. They know what glass is. My beads will last until they are all dead and buried with them. I could go dig up my beads in fifty years and trade them again."

"Uh." Zoe rolled her eyes. "Those Indian beads you have are hand-carved, delicately carved. There is no price for human artistry."

Marguerite reached for something under her bed. Pausing, she looked right at Zoe. "How do you suppose glass is made? Glass blowing is an artform, too."

Taking a doll from a box, she handed it to Slainie. "We've been making these."

Holding a small boy doll in her hands, Slainie inspected its pants, which were neatly folded at the bottom. The boy also wore a vest held shut with a button. Marguerite handed her another doll, a girl. She hadn't been dressed yet, but her face was finished—and meticulously. She had eyebrows, a nose and a smiling mouth shaded light pink. Then Slainie saw how straight and equally-spaced the stitching was across the top of her head.

Slainie gazed at Marguerite in wonderment. "Would you teach me to sew like you? My mother would be truly surprised."

Marguerite responded immediately, as if this misunderstanding was an insult. "Come, I don't sew. That's Zoe's part. I paint the faces, make their jewelry, do their hair."

"Let's start now." Zoe handed Slainie a needle and two round pieces of cloth. "That will be a doll's head. Ok? You're going to do an invisible stitch around the edge of that circle. Leave an inch hole at the bottom for stuffing. Hey, you want someone to walk you home? You could stay later."

"Actually, I have to leave soon," Slainie said. "I'm going toward Dyckesville anyway."

"Why Dyckesville?" asked Zoe.

"Not really Dyckesville. I'm going to meet Marie."

"Doesn't Marie live on the other side of your house?"

"She does. She isn't at home."

Marguerite tilted her head so she could catch Slainie's down-turned eyes. "Where is she then? Where are you actually going?"

"She's going to be in Robinsonville." Slainie turned her face away from Marguerite.

"You're going to that chapel, aren't you? The one where that unsightly woman gives sermons to the crowds?"

"Marguerite!" Zoe gave Marguerite's leg a mild kick. "There are more agreeable ways to refer to someone who isn't handsome like yourself."

Marguerite grumbled and continued to place blue beads in a pile on her pillow.

"Have you met Adele?" asked Zoe. "She is quite nice."

"A few times. She goes to Marie's house often."

"You don't believe her, do you?" asked Marguerite.

"Believe what?"

"So, you haven't heard her outlandish tale? The one about the woman hovering in the woods? She says the Virgin Mary gave her a mission. I just can't believe it—she's illiterate, can't read a word, and terribly uneducated in all else. Why would the Mother of God send a peasant to do anything for her?"

"She told you about it?" Slainie asked.

Zoe slid onto the floor next to Slainie to peek at her stitches. "Of course. She's been to the farm. Even during the winter she came once a week."

Marguerite sat up straight. "The woman makes me uncomfortable. I didn't much like her coming here."

"She helped us, though. She trimmed the hooves on the sheep and fed the pigs. A few times, she even came early to milk for us," said Zoe.

"She did do that." Marguerite's posture loosened.

Slainie handed Zoe the doll head that she had been stitching. After inspecting it, Zoe looked at Slainie with an eyebrow raised.

"I told you. I can't hide my stitches," said Slainie.

"The stitch is called an 'invisible stitch.' Its whole purpose is to hide your stitches!" Zoe bent over with laughter. "Don't worry. You come back and we'll figure this out."

The men were gone when Slainie walked back downstairs. The table had been cleared, and Mrs. Allard had placed a vase of flowers on top of a lace runner. The white and yellow blooms had been arranged to spill out evenly. *Tidy Mrs. Allard.* Slainie sniffed their sweet fragrance before she walked out the door.

CHAPTER EIGHT

The Chapel

1860 / 11 years before the fire

THE SUN SHONE directly overhead when Slainie began her hike to the chapel. At a fork in the trail, she stripped some bark off a tree to mark where she had turned, in case she couldn't remember her way back. After walking another thirty minutes, she heard the high tone of children singing. Stepping off the trail into thick underbrush, she tip-toed between branches until she could finally see into a clearing.

Marie would be at the chapel, but Slainie wouldn't seek her out. She wasn't going to stumble into the clearing in front of everyone either. Some indescribable force was drawing her, like a current pulling a leaf down river. Without an explanation for why she was there, Slainie hoped to enter the chapel unnoticed. But what if Adele saw her? Would Adele try to get her to pray or talk or something else?

Slainie lurked behind the trees for a time, her heart pounding in her ears. Eventually, she decided to take a hesitant step, and then another and another, until she had a clearer view. She sat down and peered through the low branches. A few men were taking bites of their pork pies on a log. A woman was quietly crying at the door of the chapel. Across the clearing, another woman sat on a stump in the shade of a large maple tree while six singing children fidgeted on the ground in front of her.

A little boy in a wool sweater bounced on a stump. "Tell us, *s'il vous plait*. Please, tell us again the story!"

A girl with pigtails waved her arms in excitement. "Tell us of the *la belle femme*, the beautiful woman. We want to hear the story, Mademoiselle Pauline."

Slainie soon realized no welcoming party would rush to greet her. It was nothing so formal as that. Parting the branches, she stepped out of the woods. When she reached the chapel, she crept along the outer wall, peered around the door frame, and saw just how small the chapel really was. There was no way to enter unnoticed. *Marie did say it was the size of a wagon bed.*

At the front, a mantel shelf with one picture hanging above it drew Slainie's gaze. Marie knelt with several other children. Adele knelt behind them in her dusty black robe, arms out, as if she was ushering them toward the picture on the wall. Inside the dark wooden frame stood a lady veiled in white. She held her blue cloak open, and her heart burned with fire underneath. Wearing a tender smile, she pointed to her heart. Slainie thought it strange that the lady in the picture didn't look like she was in pain. The lady's dark eyes gazed ahead toward some unknown thing and convinced Slainie that they were fixed on something beautiful. She stared at the image for a minute, feeling drawn to her without knowing why.

Then, from under the maple tree, the children exclaimed in unison as Pauline started their long-awaited story. Every one of them perched straight and tall on their bottoms.

"The lady in the trees told Adele she was being idle. Adele thought she had done God's will by coming to America, but the lady said that she hadn't made herself busy with God's tasks like all of her friends had."

The children mouthed some of the words in the story, intensifying the woman's lively intonation.

"But, Adele did not know what more she could do, and she asked the lady to tell her. What did the lady say?" Pauline leaned toward the children with wide, twinkling eyes. "The beautiful Queen of Heaven said, 'Gather the children in this wild country and teach them what they must know for salvation.'"

One of the girls eagerly blinked her sweet blue eyes at Pauline. "What look did the lady possess, Mademoiselle Pauline?"

"Oh, she was radiant. She came as light—blinding light. But, then the light began to take on a shape, and it was her. It was the Virgin Mary. She was floating between these two trees here." Pauline turned around to point to the maple tree and the hemlock tree behind her. Throwing their heads back, the children scanned the star-shaped leaves and pine needles intermixed above them.

"She was clothed in a dazzling white dress with a yellow sash tied round her waist. Over her long, golden hair, she wore most beautifully a crown of stars. Adele tells us that she could scarcely stand to look at her, so lovely and radiant she was."

Listening attentively, Slainie sat with her back against the side of the chapel. A woman in a red shawl climbed to her feet and approached Pauline and the curious children.

"Good heavens, you tell some story," said the woman. "Really, I have enjoyed it, and the children are so delighted to hear it again and again. But, it is only a tale, right? One about a lost soul returned from the dead. A ghost, maybe? That's more probable than the virgin come down from heaven."

The children, who had turned to look at the woman, resumed their questioning stare at Pauline.

"I know it sounds incredible." Pauline walked toward the

woman in the shawl, speaking serenely. "It takes such faith to believe. Our Lady knew it would, so she told Adele, 'Blessed are they who have faith yet do not see.' This our Lord has said also."

A man walked up, smoothing his wild hair, and then pointed at Pauline. "This God, the one you always talk about, he ain't goin' ta come here, ta these woods here. There ain't nothin' here ta see but ten cabins and a whole lotta trees." With great enthusiasm, his arms fanned out to illustrate the expanse of trees around them. "And, what really done make sense is this lady being the one who'd come anyhow, if the old man was really after sumptin from us."

One of the younger girls at Pauline's feet started playing with another girl's hair bow. Pauline held out her hands, and the girl leapt up into her lap. While Slainie waited for Pauline to respond, two men came from behind the chapel, and stood near the children.

"Sir, my name is Philippe Lafont. I wish to help with these questions you are putting to Ms. LaPlante."

Before the words registered in her mind, Slainie recognized the man's leisurely gait. *Did he say Lafont?* Then his sincere tone sunk in. *Oh goodness. That's my father.* Slainie shrunk behind her hands to avoid being seen.

Her father approached—merely twenty feet away—shaking hands with the wild-haired man. Marie's father strode alongside him. Slainie shuddered. It made sense that Marie's father was there if Marie was. *How silly of me! Of course Mr. Martin would see me here.* Slainie would have run back into the woods had she not been so intensely interested in what her father would say.

The man continued with his question. "What's he—well, what's this God wantin' from us anyhow?"

"That's not really how we've heard Ms. LaPlante or Ms. Brise explain it," said Mr. Lafont.

"Then, how'd they put it?"

Though he turned slightly, Mr. Lafont's back still faced Slainie. "You said God was after something from us, and maybe He is, but the way I see it, He wants to give us something. You could call it a warning."

"But, I was sayin', there ain't no reason He done jus' come himself. No reason this Mary should come instead."

Stepping next to Mr. Lafont, Marie's father now shook the man's hand, not letting go until he had finished explaining. "I suppose she *wanted* to come. She wanted the honor of it. Not honor for herself, I'm not saying that. She only wanted to do the work of her Son, Jesus."

The man scowled. "How's that a thing you'd know? How you supposin' you'd know the thoughts of people who are dead?"

Slainie's father, whom she had never heard speak of religion, shrugged and turned to Pauline. The slight woman was now surrounded by a crowd. It seemed this little debate was of great interest to many of the chapel visitors.

The woman in a red shawl began to question Pauline again. "Say we imagine for one minute that this vision was not just a ghost wandering about. Let's say it was indeed Mary. It was the mother of Jesus. She is not God. She does not have the powers of God. Why, isn't she a ghost herself, just another dead person?"

Yes, the inquisitive man nodded vigorously and the children whispered to each other, but Pauline remained undeterred.

"Have you heard of the Immaculate Conception?"

The man's eyes slowly scanned the faces around him, as if he was embarrassed for not knowing, but the woman in the shawl just said "no" with a sneer.

Pauline smiled and walked back to her stump. "It's a title, a sort of name for the Virgin Mary. In fact, our Most Holy Father in Rome recently declared the Immaculate Conception a dogma.

It means that Mary never inherited the sin of humanity, the original sin. The vessel that carried our Lord had to be pure and clean,
so she was purer even than a baby just born to life. It has been
divinely revealed and cannot be denied."

Scoffing, the woman in the shawl looked for agreement in
those around her. "Better than us then."

"Yes. She is unlike us in that way. The angel in the Bible
called her 'full of grace,'" said Pauline, joy brightening her face as
she squeezed the child in her lap.

The disbelieving woman spoke with those around her now,
and Slainie wished she could hear what was being said. The
woman gestured to the sky with great passion, then to Pauline,
then to the sky again.

Straining to yell above the noise, a down-at-heel old man
stood up, saying, "What's any of this mean to us, to the lot of us
working ourselves to death?"

"It means she loves us. Purely," said Pauline, "and she's qual-
ified to be a messenger for God."

"These ideas, they all come from Rome." The woman in the
shawl was yelling now. "They all come from the imagination of
your leader. They're not in the Bible."

"Now, wait a minute." Slainie's father stepped in front of
Pauline, but she walked around him, and said, "I see where you
are coming from now. You're a Methodist, true?"

"It doesn't matter what I am," said the woman. "Yours is still
a church full of scandal and lies."

"People are never perfect, not even those who have led the
Church. It doesn't make what they say untrue." Pauline reached
out to touch the woman's hand. "It seems fair to point out that
you only have the Bible because of Catholics. It was Catholics
who gathered the stories of the Israelites, of Jesus and his apostles. Those are the stories in your Bible. It was a Catholic named

Jerome who spent his life translating the Bible into Latin, just so
more of the faithful could read it for themselves. And it was medi-
eval monks—Catholic monks—who guarded the Holy Texts and
transcribed them when churches and monasteries were being pil-
laged. Given all of this, who better than Catholics to tell us what
is in the Bible and what it means?"

The woman shook her head violently, as if she refused to hear
the words. Taking a deep breath, Slainie's father walked over to
the woman again. "Don't you know the first pope was the apostle
Peter?"

Slainie still sat unnoticed against the chapel. *How does he
know this?*

The woman, raising her arms like a self-proclaimed prophet,
turned to the crowd and shouted over the din. "Listen all! Hear
the truth of the Methodist Reformed Church. Popish Rome sent
this woman to gain rule over us. Rome wants to subdue all people
under its doctrines and control. But we live in a free land now."

Slainie's mouth dropped. She hadn't been prepared for the
confusion of ideas being presented to her. Now she wanted to
find Marie.

The inquisitive man stepped away from the woman in the red
shawl. Several other men watched her with furrowed brows. The
woman who had been crying near the chapel now mingled in the
crowd, clutching her tissue to her cheek. Pauline only bowed her
head. Then a familiar figure eased past Slainie.

Adele walked a straight line toward the woman, her black
cloak swaying in the dirt with every step.

The woman howled her final plea. "You will all fall prey if
you believe in this vision, this supposed miracle, that the mother
of Jesus should be worshipped and praised with love that is
reserved only for the Lord. You'll bring the destruction of this
new country."

Adele calmly placed a hand on her arm. "Let us speak in the chapel."

Jerking away, the woman inspected Adele, who most certainly looked like a nun in her long tunic and rope belt.

"An emissary to your majesty, the pope?" the woman said to her.

"No, only a friend. Come."

Reluctantly, the woman turned to follow Adele. She avoided brushing even an elbow with anyone in the crowd. Slainie wanted to join them. She considered sneaking to the door of the chapel to listen to them talking inside. She was angry, jealous that this huge world of knowledge existed without her having been allowed to enter.

When she turned back to the crowd, Slainie saw that everyone else had turned to watch Adele and the woman go. Everyone, including her father. Facing her now, his gaze locked onto hers for several seconds. She froze. *He's upset with me. He'll tell mother, and I'll never see the chapel again. Maybe he doesn't see me. Maybe he'll think he imagined me here.*

Before he could approach her, Slainie jumped to her feet, sprinted around the chapel and dashed into the woods. Bristles and thorns bit the skin under her skirt. She dodged the giant roots of trees until she found the trail again. Then, hoping to beat her father home, she ran and ran. She didn't know what she would do once she arrived, probably just go to bed and hope her father would keep it all a secret. She winced as the bag of her mother's mending began to rub her shoulder raw.

Where is the tree I stripped of bark? Where is the turn? She scanned the woods. Soon, it became harder and harder to see anything—to see the trees or their branches as anything but one dark mass. Everything turned grey, and soon a half moon provided the only light.

Slainie was desperately lost.

I must be near Dyckesville by now. If I could just see something to guide me. Anything. She couldn't find a light in the trees, a fire, a lantern, a whining of chickens—anything to steer her to a house. In her frenzied fear, she thought of Indians and recalled the stories her brothers had told her—the ones they tried to scare her with—of the women and children the Dakota tribe had chased into a slough just across the river in Minnesota Territory.

She opened her eyes to stop the visions, but they played themselves upon the dark. Huge, strong men in red paint. Men with jewelry made from bones. Women adorned with giant beaded necklaces, yelling at settlers and hitting them with clubs as they crawled along the soggy ground. Babies crying, mothers wailing, and men yelling out for their loved ones.

Exhausted, she hugged a tree with both arms and slid down its trunk. Though prickly, the cold ground on her cheek comforted her. Then with her back up against the tree, she curled into a ball and cried. Off in the distance, coyotes howled, and she fell asleep in the dirt.

CHAPTER NINE

Acorns and Pigweed

1860 / 11 years before the fire

SLAINIE HAD QUITE a row with her mother the morning after the chapel incident. As Mrs. Lafont erupted, Slainie hid her face in her father's shoulder and sobbed. She didn't dare to meet her mother's eyes. Her clothes were torn and soiled with dirt, and she ached as though she had been pummeled by horses or beaten like a rug with a battling stick.

Outside, Slainie's brothers shuffled below the window. *Oh, no. They're listening to all of this. It's just one more thing they'll tease me about.* While the boys whispered and snickered to one another, Mrs. Lafont gave no sign she noticed.

"Your father and your brothers were up all night looking for you. The neighbors sent their dogs out looking for you. Me and Modette, we couldn't sleep a wink."

"I'm sorry, Maman."

"I was just sick thinking you'd been eaten by wolves or kidnapped by Indians!"

"I'm sorry, Maman."

"Mr. Detienne said you were shivering in the dirt when he

found you—only had a clue to your whereabouts because of a tree he found stripped of bark. You were crying in your sleep and all the way in Dyckesville." Mrs. Lafont slapped her hands hard on the table. "What on earth were you doing there? I can't find the reason for it."

Still lying against her father's chest, Slainie turned to face her mother. "Please forgive me, Maman."

Mrs. Lafont sneered. "I'm puttin' you to work. My forgiveness is in keeping you in this cabin at all. There will be no more wandering the woods. No visits. No deliveries. Did you even think about the possibility of your own death out there?"

"Margot, I think our girl is shaken enough. Maybe she should go be alone, so she can calm herself." Slainie's father slowly lifted her head off of his chest.

Mrs. Lafont huffed. "*Allez*, go. But, don't you make one footprint in those woods, not for a few weeks, maybe a month or two. Your work is here. As for your deliveries, your siblings can do them."

At this last statement, Vincent and Jacques groaned just beyond the window. Modette, who lay in her bunk, pursed her lips.

Suddenly standing, Mrs. Lafont hollered, "You boys get to the garden now. I want every weed gone." She turned around. "Modette, those chickens need seed."

"*Oui*, yes, Maman," the boys replied in unison, then meandered across the yard.

When Modette had moved off to the shed, Slainie slunk to their small front porch and sat on the bench. Though the porch was only a small rectangle of dirt, they often swept it free of pine needles and rocks, and it was in the shade of the house. It was a nice spot to look out on the trees. A thinking spot. With her arms around her upturned knees, Slainie watched one of her brothers take up a bucket and the other whack at the soil with the pointy end of a pick mattock. Slainie's mind remained on her parents and their conversation just inside the door.

"What was she doing out there so far, Philippe?"

"She was seeing the chapel at Robinsonville."

"The chapel of that miracle woman? I don't want Slainie listening to that lunacy. I knew she was seeing that woman at Marie Martin's place, and I was stupid to allow it."

"Margot, *ecoute*. Listen. Our girl is a good girl. She does her work. She minds well what you say. Even so, you know she is smart. You know she needs more. She needs to seek answers to the questions she has, in her own way . . . and you may not be able to stop her."

Worried her father had angered her mother, Slainie released her knees and peeked into the window. Mrs. Lafont stood at the sink up to her elbows in dish water. "You too have been poisoned by these stories. Have you been to that chapel? Have you seen it?"

Mr. Lafont turned his head away from his wife's contemptuous glare as her hands continued washing the plates. While he avoided answering her, dishes collided in the sink and the pick mattock hacked away at soil between the rows of peas, breaking the silence.

Finally, Mr. Lafont's courage returned. "Yes. I have seen it."

Mrs. Lafont gasped. "You and her. The two of you—you're always looking for more than what is right in front of you. I need that girl here. Her life is here inside this house. She needs to learn her way. She must be ready to be someone's wife and—"

"*Ma chérie, te calmer*. Calm down, my dear. You worry so much. She sees the work you do every day. She knows life demands hard work from her. If she does her work, why do you mind if she has her head somewhere else while she does it?"

When the clanking of dishes stopped, Slainie knew her mother was really mad, probably too mad for words, probably bracing herself on the sink while she fought the urge to holler. Then, to her surprise, Slainie heard weeping.

"I won't hear of this," Mrs. Lafont wailed. "She is not to go to that chapel. As far as I'm concerned, she is not to go off our land. That's what I told her, and I tell it to you again. You let me raise my daughter. I already lost one."

Mr. Lafont's voice hushed to a weary whisper. "*Ma chérie. You are not going to lose this one.*"

Slainie burst into tears, and her brothers looked up from their labor. Hating for them to see her, she ran behind the house and sat on the woodpile. With a calming rustle, the wind glided through the budding branches of the forest in front of her. It blew through her hair, and her sobs weakened to sniffles. She mulled over her predicament. *Why am I crying?* She sifted through her emotions realizing it wasn't about the loss of her sister or the loss of her freedom. She was so used to her mother's coldness she'd actually believed her mother despised her. Today, Slainie learned she didn't.

There it is. She's only worried for me? Is that really why she's so mean? She could just tell me that. If she told me, I could convince her I'm ready to learn. I'm going to do what she wants. I always try to. Always will. I know I can make her proud of me.

With new clarity, Slainie recalled how single-minded her mother was about leaving Belgium. Their hut had been so small. Moreover, it had a roof leak and a dangerously hot pipe that carried the smoke out. It was dirty, drafty and soot-filled. *Mother only wanted to give us something more than all of that. A better place. A future.*

In Belgium, when he wasn't away for work, Slainie's father would sit on the rug with his children and tell stories about people he had seen on the streets. He told jokes they'd heard a thousand times. "Why wouldn't the villagers sell the barber any pets?" The children pretended not to know. "Because he was always cutting his hare." Slainie and her siblings laughed, only to humor Papa. "I complimented a farmer today," he would say. "I told him he was outstanding in his field." After a sip of warm milk, they would all lie back and close their eyes. Mr. Lafont would hum them a happy tune until his voice faltered and he fell asleep.

Mr. Lafont tried to lighten everyone's burden all the time. Making people happy was his way of taking care of them. *Maybe Mother's way is preparing us for the worst. Maybe all her worrying and criticism come from her heart too.*

As Slainie's mind flowed from one memory to the next, her father rounded the corner of the house. He scratched his gray beard and walked past the wood pile.

"Come on, Slay. Walk with me."

Wiping her eyes, she caught up. He put his arm around her shoulders and kissed her head.

As they entered the woods, he inspected the ground, stopping abruptly to pick a small plant. It looked like something Slainie had seen her brothers pull from the garden and burn.

"Papa, what are you doing?"

"See this? It's called 'purslane.'" He took a bite off one of its little plump leaves. "It's sour, but refreshing. Try it."

She took the little plant in her hands. The leaves were smooth, but didn't look good to eat. She nibbled it.

"Does it taste better if you cook it?"

He smiled and began walking again.

"Your mother was cutting that up, boiling it, and feeding it to us for months when we first arrived."

A few minutes later, he bent down and picked up an acorn.

"This is an acorn."

"I know. I have seen an acorn before. I have seen a squirrel too."

Her father laughed.

"But do you remember eating these also? Your mother has made flour out of them."

She looked down at the piles of acorns littering the forest floor and realized she had never paid attention to her mother in the kitchen.

"She loves you. You know that," said Mr. Lafont.

Slainie sniffled and a sob rose in her chest.

"Your mother, she thinks she can control everything in life. She is hard on you, I know, but that's because she worries about you."

Slainie let the acorn roll out of her hand. "I just want to make her happy."

Mr. Lafont started walking again.

"Why didn't you tell her you were at the chapel? I mean, before today," Slainie asked.

"Your mother takes a good amount of time. She doesn't see things as quickly as you. I've been going to the chapel for months. When I think she is ready, I will tell her everything I have learned."

He picked up another acorn.

"Everything?"

"Yes. See, it started that I was just lonely, working all the time, never seeing anyone. Back home in Belgium, I worked around people every day. Here, only a few men cross my path, and even then, not every day. Other days, I only have the silence of the land for company, but the chapel is drawing people from all the Belgian settlements, even Germans and Irish. I began hiking there before work. After a while, I began thinking about what the women there said. I couldn't help but make a decision about the whole thing."

Slainie picked a new plant from the dirt. "A decision about what?"

"That's called lamb's quarter. You boil it."

She stared at him, waiting for a response.

"It's also called 'goosefoot' or 'pigweed.' I have heard some call it 'fat hen.' Our Indian friends showed us that one."

"Papa?"

"*Ouais.* Yeah. My decision. I decided . . . I believe it."

"You believe the stories?"

"*Ouais.*"

"Do you believe it was the Mother of God? What about Jesus? Him too?"

"*Oui.* Yes."

"Pa? What about church? Shouldn't we be going if you believe all of this?"

"We should."

"But we can't, can we?"

"No. It's a big sacrifice to ask of your mother. It takes all day to get to and from the church. Your mother isn't ready. She's still mourning your sister—actually she hasn't even begun to mourn for Cecilia. If we push her, she will only become a stone. Do you understand?"

Slainie nodded. She gazed down the trail, remembering the room in Kaukauna and how small her sister looked when they wrapped her in a quilt. She felt the pit of her stomach tighten when the memory of Cecilia's tiny arm lying limp against the bedside flashed through her mind.

Mr. Lafont picked all of the lamb's quarters he could find. "When she is ready, I will bring her to the chapel. We will all go together. You, me, mother, Modette and the boys. I promise."

Slainie relaxed into a patch of greenery on the side of the trail. Feeling achy, she remembered the roots and rocks on which she had slept the night before.

"It shouldn't be long," Mr. Lafont said, scraping dirt from

under his nails. "Soon, I will ask your mother to show a little faith. The settlers are planning to build a bigger chapel next spring. The one there now is always full to the gills with people. They come at all hours, and I should really do whatever I can to help. With your mother's blessing, that is."

Slainie snagged a handful of lamb's quarters before standing. "But you're too busy to help, Papa."

"You might be right, but I believe I can help in the evening, after I work the fields. I won't be around much, but I promise, I will bring news back for you. We can go picking plants for mother, and I will tell you everything that happens."

She hugged him. "Oh, I would like that. I don't think I'm going to be able to go myself. Maybe ever."

Mr. Lafont wrapped his arms around her, lifted, and spun her in a circle.

"You know your mother. She loves you. Just don't forget that."

Slainie laughed, as her toes dragged in the dirt.

"I won't, Papa."

CHAPTER TEN

Papa's Confession

1860 / 11 years before the fire

TRUE TO HER word, Mrs. Lafont assigned the boys to deliveries and Slainie to laundry duty—the worst chore in the house. Being stronger and older, it took her brothers only two days to complete the whole laundry process. For Slainie, it took four.

On the morning of the first day, she hauled water to the house, trekking through the woods to the stream, where every squeak or creak spooked her. Her fear had only grown since that nightmarish evening she spent against a tree trunk imagining Indian war stories and carnivorous wolves. She still didn't know how to handle it. Hauling water took all morning. In the afternoon, she boiled the clothes in a pot over the fire and left them overnight to soak in soap.

On the second day, Slainie removed the dripping items from their pots and beat them with a battling stick. When she finished, her entire body was doused in sweat and soapy water, and she rested for lunch. Afterwards, she pushed each piece of clothing up and down, side-to-side, up and down and side-to-side, on the ridges of a washboard. Finally, after hiking to the creek for more water, she rinsed everything and hung the wet, heavy items on the line. By then, she was ready to sink into the ground, but this was just the end of the second day. The other half of the laundry waited for her. By the time Slainie completed the whole process, it was the end of the fourth day.

On the fifth day, she wanted to sleep forever. She ached all over and stayed longer in bed to stretch, reaching her arms up over her head, pointing her toes, flexing her calves, and hugging her knees to her chest. It took an hour for everything to loosen up so she could get back to work again. Besides laundry, she still had to make and mend clothing with her mother. The walks with her father were the only respite she had. He passed along messages from Marie, Marguerite, and Zoe. Even their brother Joseph had said that he "hoped to see her again soon."

Slainie's imprisonment continued through summer and fall. When winter came, the wind and snow stopped the laundry train. In her boredom, warming herself near the stove, Slainie considered the severity of her punishment, wondering what had been the real reason for it. Was her mother afraid that she would get lost again, maybe die in the woods? Or was she afraid Slainie would go back to the chapel and come home telling her that she believed too?

As soon as spring came, construction of the new chapel at Robinsonville started. Mr. Lafont kept his promise to share all of the exciting developments with Slainie. He told her that an old friend had come to visit: the priest from Bay Settlement, Father Daems, the priest who had buried Cecilia in Kaukauna. Slainie remembered him fondly.

"The settlers were hoping he would give them a speech, but he spoke very little. He didn't help erect the chapel either. Mostly, he just wandered through the crowds asking questions about Adele."

Slainie's father took a bucket from her and crouched in the sandy bank of the stream.

After filling her own bucket with water, Slainie turned toward the cabin. "Why was he there?"

"I haven't any idea. He acted like he was investigating something, the way he looked at people. He wasn't like I remembered him at all."

Water sloshed against Slainie's leg as she stopped and spun around. Brow furrowed, concern spread across her face.

"Do you mean investigating Adele? But why?"

"Father Daems came to America with other missionaries two years before Adele arrived. I'm certain they know each other, but I don't believe they are friends. Father Daems doesn't trust the apparition story, and someone in the church sent him to the chapel. It's difficult to tell where he stands, because he still performs the sacraments for Adele's students. She travels with them to his church in Green Bay."

Hefting her bucket, Slainie continued down the well-trodden trail. "Was I baptized, Papa?"

"Indeed, you were. In Belgium."

"But, I don't know what that means. *Why* was I baptized?"

As he strolled behind Slainie, Mr. Lafont suddenly reached for her bucket with his free hand. "Let's see. The way Adele tells it, you received the Spirit of God. It cleansed your soul of the sin you were born with. You know, I was baptized too. And, before we left Belgium, I dressed in my best clothes every Sunday. At least, when I wasn't working."

Mr. Lafont glanced down at his clogs, now caked with mud. "Me and your mother went to a few classes in a church . . . Sint Lambertuskerk, it was. We had all of you baptized there as babies."

"I heard Adele telling Marie about baptism and . . . Wait! You must tell me, Papa. Do you really eat the body of a man?"

"It's not just *some* man. It's Jesus," said her father. "I took the Eucharist every week as a boy. I ate it up, sat back down, and horsed around with my brothers. I never thought a thing about it."

Slainie sat on a log. Pa rolled another one close and sat too. He plunked down a bucket between Slainie's feet.

"Only now do I know I was eating the Body of my Lord. His life goes into me, so I can become more like Him."

"What? That's not what they do in church, is it? You *are* eating a person? That sounds . . . apologies, Papa, but it sounds gross."

"No, Slainie. Listen. It doesn't make much sense. Maybe that's why so many people don't bother with it. Adele told us to start praying that it'll make sense. It's not flesh. I mean, it won't look like flesh."

"It sounds like magic."

"It's not magic. It's a miracle," said Mr. Lafont. "There's so much I want to tell you. You have to go to confession first. You can't just eat it whenever you want. It's there, at Mass, but you can't just go to Mass and sit there either. You have to be there with your heart and mind."

"Adele told Marie about confession too. Have you done it?"

Mr. Lafont looked off in the distance. Slainie waited until he finally turned back to her. "Here, I think this will help you understand."

Then, her father became quite serious. Yes, he had been to confession. Slainie didn't think her father could have any sins, but he told her that he had purposely caused the garden to die back in Belgium, just by neglecting it. Then he lied to Mrs. Lafont about it. He knew it could never grow enough to feed them all, and he wanted to be freed from laboring over it. He told Slainie he had neglected her brothers, avoided them even. He should have disciplined them better, shown them how to be good men. He had even stolen food from a nearby farm. In those early days in America, he had filched apples from some trees and meat off a drying line.

Slainie pooh-poohed the idea. "That seems such a small thing. We were nearly starving."

"I was stealing. It was a sin, and I needed to confess it. It kept me from communion. It kept me from knowing Him."

"Knowing Jesus?" Slainie interrupted.

"Yes." Her father sighed. "How can I make you understand? When I sin, it's like betraying a friend. Jesus is a person. He's God, but a person, just like you and me. When you betray a friend, you have pushed your friend away. In this case, that friend is also your God and the One who died for you."

Slainie mindlessly nudged the tiny heads of bluebells in the flower bed near her. She watched them sway as she listened to her father.

Mr. Lafont took her hand. "Is this all making sense for you?" Slainie peered up at him and shrugged.

"Here's why Adele is so important." He closed his eyes for a moment, as if steeling himself against shocking news. "Do you remember when we first got here? You were six, maybe seven. We were all sending letters home about this land, and almost over-night hundreds of new settlers showed up with our letters in their hands. Remember Mr. Dehousse and his wife?"

"*Ouais.* They stayed with us for a few months."

"Everyone had someone staying with them. It was madness."

"Then I remember the Dehousses were just gone one morn-ing. You told us they found a home in a different settlement."

Mr. Lafont met Slainie's gaze. "See, Slay, they never left. They had actually died, that night, in their sleep. The disease took them so fast . . . we had to bury them. Carried them from the house before you children ever awakened."

"What? How?"

"They brought cholera from Belgium."

"Were we sick, too, Papa?"

"No. You weren't sick, but it's a wonder we didn't all get sick. We never caught the tuberculosis when your sister had it, but then to survive cholera . . . to survive twice? Boy, it's some kind of miracle. People were going to bed fine and lying dead by morning. All over Wisconsin, all over everywhere. The point is, these people were being buried out in the woods. Just thrown inside shallow holes and that was that. Now we know they should have received a sacrament before they died. Actually, they should have received it right when they became ill. A priest has to give it to them. They should have received confession too, and the Eucharist, just one last time, before they died. They deserved a final chance to make that choice."

"Which choice?" asked Slainie.

"To choose God. To choose to give up their sins and pride and be good men before they meet their Maker. They should have received a final blessing at their burial. But, they didn't receive any of this. No one thought about these things. Fine Catholics we were. We had no idea what aid the church had to give in a man's final hours."

Slowly shaking his head, Pa looked at his hands.

"You didn't do anything wrong, Papa. You don't think you did a bad thing?"

"It was all bad," he said, "but it couldn't be helped. Now . . . with Adele here . . . it can be."

CHAPTER ELEVEN

Barn Dance

1861 / 10 years before the fire

SLAINIE didn't have a chance to talk with her father again for several weeks. He was gone making benches at the chapel. Back on laundry duty, her brothers continued to taunt her. "How's a person as strong as a pine needle bring up all that water? Who's helping you? Those big scary Indians?" Ignoring them, Slainie pushed the clothing down harder on the washboard.

At the end of May, Mr. Lafont took Slainie on what he called their final herb-gathering trip. They strolled down the trail not saying much until Slainie began to think he was upset about something.

"Papa, I didn't tell anyone what you told me about the meat and the apples and letting the garden die. I wouldn't. I promise."

He halted and turned to her. "You're worried I'm upset with you?" He laughed. "The idea never crossed my mind."

"Then, what, Papa? Why is this our last walk? Why are you so quiet?"

With a playful, sly smile, he whispered, "I forgot to tell you. Mother is letting you come out this Saturday."

Slainie stepped back and stared at him. His smile widened.

"Truly?" She squeezed his hands. "No joking? I never asked to go out. Are you certain?"

"I am certain. There's going to be a barn dance to celebrate the completion of the new chapel. Adele and her friends will be there. The Allards are coming. Marie's family. The Petinoits. Besides, I think your mother wants you out of the house, and by now she *must* be softening toward you again."

Full of excitement, Slainie smiled so broadly her face hurt. She hadn't seen her friends since last spring, almost a whole year ago. She tried to keep from dancing around the house as she prepared for bed. Over the next few days, she didn't speak a word of it for fear that her mother would change her mind. Slainie discreetly scrounged in dressers and trunks to pull together an ensemble to wear.

Only a few girls in the settlement had anything fancy. Even the thread they used to make their dresses had to be made by them first. Slainie had no time to make something new. Fortunately, she discovered a rose-colored dress that her mother had made as a practice piece. Little white embroidered flowers lined the collar. Two thin strips of lace ran from Slainie's neck down to her waistline. In between the strips, ten beautiful shell buttons glistened white.

Although Modette wasn't attending, she helped Slainie braid her hair all tight and tidy. Modette obeyed their mother in all things, and because Mrs. Lafont abhorred that chapel, she chose to stay home and spend the evening sewing.

When the oxen trotted up outside, Mrs. Lafont sat kneading dough at the table. Slainie mumbled "goodbye" to her mother, who shooed her away with the flick of her flour-coated hand.

Outside, Mr. Lafont lugged his liquor kegs onto Mr. Allard's wagon. "Boys! *Viennent!* Come!" Vincent and Jacques came bursting out of the house. "You two get the rest of these kegs up here."

In the driver's seat, Mr. Allard nodded to Slainie. "*Bonjour, mademoiselle.* Hello, Miss. Hey, Joseph, give her your hand."

Joseph hopped down from the wagon bench and got on one knee. Slainie hesitated.

"Come on, Slay. Use my knee. Climb in."

"Slay!" hollered Henri, from the bench. "We're glad to have you back. Don't worry, Vincent. You can still come and fold our laundry for us."

Vincent stepped toward Henri, speaking low and menacingly. "When you least expect it, that's when you're going to get it."

"Is that right?" Joseph strode up next to Henri.

"That's enough," Mr. Lafont said, and his boys climbed into the wagon, dangling their legs over the edge.

Mr. Lafont clapped his hand on Mr. Allard's back. "François, this is going to be a good night."

"You don't say, Philippe. You think this batch's finally ready? Because I've been waiting for it!" Clicking his tongue, Mr. Allard steered his oxen onto the road, now only dimly lit by the setting sun.

"It's ready. You may have to drink fifty or sixty mugs of it, but eventually it'll do the trick."

With their backs against the kegs, Henri and Joseph told Slainie about the mishaps she had missed at their farm. During one unfortunate event, Henri was preparing manure for ploughing, and the pile tumbled off the wagon and buried him underneath.

His lip curling in disgust, Henri tried to explain. "It hadn't been watered enough." Slainie's laughter rolled on and on. Joseph and the Lafont boys split their sides.

"It was manure for Henri and ewe's milk for Marguerite," Joseph added. "She was teaching a new farm hand how to milk.

The udder was so full and swollen, it was terrible to control. Marguerite took a spray in the face, in her hair, everywhere. She stormed into the house, mad as a hatter."

When the wagon jerked out of a deep rut, Slainie's head slammed against a keg. Joseph rushed to cup the back of her head, checking for a welt or a wound.

Henri nudged her. "She's tougher than that."

"Can't be so sure," Jacques chimed in. "Should have seen her tripping over the *smallest* buckets of water for laundry." A strange, forced bark came out of Vincent, like angry laughter.

Slainie couldn't see her brother's faces in the dark, which made ignoring them easier. "I'm all right, Joseph. Thank you."

When the wagon eased to a stop in front of the barn, half a dozen farmers came to greet them at the wagon. They shook Mr. Lafont's hand in turn and heaved kegs up on their shoulders to take inside. All the boys jumped off the wagon, but Slainie waited. She didn't want to rip her dress. Joseph had almost reached the door when he turned back and spotted her at the wagon's edge.

"What are you waiting for?" he hollered to her.

"Uhh . . . I don't think I can get myself down."

"Geez, it's only but two-and-a-half feet to the grass."

"It's this dress." Slainie lifted one side of her skirt to attempt a descent, but Joseph already approached. After she set foot on the ground, he held out his arm to lead her to the door, but she rushed ahead.

Inside the barn, men talked on hay bales, and women chattered in groups. Bits of hay fell from the ceiling where children were climbing the ladder to the loft. At the far end, the settlers band played—three men with a French horn, a banjo and a guitar. With flowing arm gestures, a lady in a purple apron sang "*Partant pour la Syrie*," a patriotic Belgian song. The singer's powerful vibrato marked the end of each phrase.

Some settlers left their places in the hay to dance. The ladies made a circle on the inside, facing the men in a wider circle. Bowing to one another, they took each other's hands. Slainie beamed as they moved in a series of spins, circle rounds and partner swaps. Elated to be in the midst of such happy clamor, she scanned the room until she caught Marie's eye. Marie came running. Laughing, the two friends jumped up and down. Soon, Zoe and Marguerite spotted Slainie and were instantly at her side.

Zoe threw her arms around Slainie. "Your pa said you were working at home for a while. What on earth could you have been working on all winter?"

"It wasn't actually work. My mother didn't want me in the woods."

Zoe frowned and looked her in the eye. "I heard you were lost. Something about going out too far, somewhere near Dyckesville. Was it the day we spoke about Sister Adele?"

"*Ouais.*" Slainie's cheeks reddened.

Marguerite hadn't changed a bit since the previous spring. She still bypassed sentimentality about anyone else's feelings. "I couldn't believe it. Why did you not find an Indian and ask him to guide you home?"

"Really, Maggie? Stop it." Zoe swatted her younger sister's arm.

"*C'est vrai*, it's true," said Slainie. "Terribly true."

Marie grabbed Slainie's arms with excitement. "There's so much to tell you. My brother has been talking to Father Daems about building a school at Holy Cross. You know what that means?" She paused with a bounce. "It means I can teach. I mean, we can teach, Zoe and I. Well, not yet. Xavier's only begun to teach English to us. Zoe knows more than I do."

"Don't forget about me." Marguerite stepped in front of Zoe, and Zoe elbowed Marguerite aside.

Marie adored her older brother and had read each of Xavier's letters from Philadelphia to Slainie whenever she visited. When Marie's family first emigrated, Xavier had stayed in Philadelphia to learn English. Then he joined his people again in the Wisconsin settlement and eventually became their mayor. He was known as a champion for the Belgian settlers. He lobbied for them, helping them attain improved roads and convincing all the Belgians to vote.

As the band broke for food and drinks, the noise abated. Two boys approached from behind Zoe—the Willem boys, Jules and Etienne. Their father operated the grist mill in Dyckesville.

Slainie leaned close to Zoe's ear. "Behind you."

The boys came around and bowed to the Allard sisters.

One of them reached out his hand. "Would you like to dance?"

"It would be my pleasure," said Zoe, walking off with him.

Frozen, Marguerite stared at the second boy, who still stood in front of her. She curtsied slightly and then turned and fled out the barn door. Looking stunned, her would-be dance partner nodded to Slainie and stalked away, like a scolded dog.

Slainie headed outside, yelling to Marguerite over a gust of wind.

"Maggie? Marguerite? Are you okay?"

When Slainie reached her, Marguerite stood with arms crossed in the cold air, gazing at the moon high over the trees. "No. I am definitely not okay. You've missed so much, being sequestered for a year. Let's see . . . Pa's mill is up. You recall that man from New York—you know, the one who put his feet up on our dinner table? Couldn't believe the nerve of that guy. Surprisingly, his offer to my pa was sincere. He helped Pa plant sixty acres of wheat."

"What about you though?"

Marguerite continued to watch the moon as if she were trying to decipher a message on its surface. "I had hoped to go back to New York. Have you heard of Singer, the sewing machines?"

"No, I haven't."

"Well, gee, Slay. You need to read up on these things." Marguerite slowly turned her head toward Slainie. "Singer's machine is going to make it easier to produce clothing for everyone, even for girls like us. I want to be in the big city when it happens. Making dolls showed me that I can create lovely things, things people really want to buy. I want to design fine clothes for people and make them on Singer's machine."

"But you'd have to leave your family, wouldn't you?"

"I would, and I was okay with that, but then Adele came back. I really thought she was crazy. Really, I did, but then I started to feel itchy, always restless, until she came again. I had questions for everything. I was entirely and surprisingly swept away."

Now that Marguerite wasn't staring at the moon, Slainie felt kind of nervous and surprised that she was so open with her. "I think I understand. I felt the same. That's why I went to the chapel and why I got lost and why . . . I haven't seen Adele since last fall."

"So, I told my mama I felt I was supposed to—well, I feel *compelled* to follow her."

"Follow? Like door to door?" Slainie sounded incredulous.

Marguerite peered off into the darkness before responding. "I guess, or wherever she goes. I just can't shake the feeling. I have waited for a different idea to sweep me away, for something to point me toward New York or marriage, anything else. It never happens."

"My papa told me that Pauline felt the same way. Didn't she say that her heart would burn with desire to follow Adele whenever she heard her speak?"

"Heart aflame . . . that's accurate." Marguerite smiled at Slainie.

"So, what does your mother say?"

"She told me it was a noble idea, but then Pa told me I wouldn't be happy in a state like that. He said I need too many things. I need too much attention."

In the moonlight, Marguerite paced, the wind whipping her hair across her face. "I know who I am. I am vain. I think myself as important as royalty. I see it. I need everything in perfect order or I . . . or I guess I'm just uncomfortable. But, I feel peace when I'm around Adele, and I think it's right to sacrifice everything for that."

She stopped and pointed at the barn. "That boy who asked me to dance? My pa has been conspiring with his parents. They're trying to push us together, to persuade me to marry."

A tear rolled down Marguerite's cheek, and she quickly flicked it away.

"Oh, no, Maggie. I'm sorry," said Slainie.

"Thank you. Never thought I'd be able to talk to you like this. You're much too quiet, you know."

For a moment, they watched dancing shadows fall upon the ground from lanterns inside the barn. Slainie thought about Marguerite. She was only absent-minded, Slainie concluded. Maybe self-centered, but not mean. She could see why the Allards wanted Marguerite to marry; she was talented in the home, and marriage would make life easier for everyone. In spite of this, Slainie knew what Marguerite wanted. She knew because she wanted it too. They sought an interior struggle, something more than a life measured solely by the labor of their hands.

Shouting erupted inside the barn, startling the girls. Marguerite grabbed Slainie's arm, and they rushed back inside. All eyes were on a short man in a clean, white shirt. His kempt appearance contradicted the insults he hurled at an older couple sitting nearby.

"You need to stop that daughter of yours! She's making a fool of you!"

A burly old man and his wife clutched each other's hands, refusing to look up at him.

"It's gone on too long! Adele has been on our property, knocking on our door. What gives her the right? What makes her so holy? She's got nothing new to say!"

Cowering on their bench, the couple wouldn't even raise their heads.

The man turned around to the stunned party-goers. "So . . . what? You're all suckered in? You believe this crazy girl?" He pushed his thumb into his chest. "Well, not me, and not the Reverend. He's going to put a stop to this or we'll—"

Two men locked arms with him, cutting him off mid-sentence and dragging him backwards from the barn. On his way out, he yelled, "They're not going to let that chapel stand!"

Slainie leaned into Marguerite and nodded to the couple that had just been verbally accosted. "What was that? Do you know those two?"

"Those are Adele's parents. That girl there, she is Adele's sister, Isabella. She was with Adele when Mary appeared."

"Was that man serious?"

"You haven't heard *this* either?" Marguerite rolled her eyes. "There are a bunch of people who don't like Adele. They think she's lying, that she's deceiving everyone."

Henri charged into the conversation. "That man should be branded on his forehead so he can't come around anymore. Can you believe him?"

"Calm down." Joseph tousled Henri's hair. "There are dozens more after him. There will always be people who oppose the truth."

"Does Adele know?" asked Slainie.

Zoe looked sorrowful. "Oh, yes. They have come—even to the chapel—with insults. But some, instead of debating with

Adele, pretend to believe just so they can set up stalls and sell their crops and handiwork to the pilgrims. Some sell alcohol too, and that is why the bishop is upset with Adele. On many occasions, the crowds have become truly wild and unruly."

"I'm going to get Pa. We need to go to the chapel right away, just in case that guy shows up there to harass people." Henri stomped off with Joseph.

Over by the hay bales, Adele's parents gazed around the barn with blank, wide eyes. Slainie watched them curiously. A crowd of concerned and sympathetic faces gathered around them, then several friends escorted them outside.

Marguerite's voice broke through the scene. "I heard yesterday the bishop threatened to excommunicate Adele if she doesn't stop telling her story."

Slainie hadn't heard this word either. "What does 'excommunicate' mean?"

"It would be awful. They would publicly declare her 'not a Catholic' anymore, and that would mean she couldn't take the Eucharist. Every priest would be forbidden to give it to her. Already, she's kneeling in the aisle at Mass when no one will give her a seat."

Henri and Joseph ran back to the girls.

"That settles it," said Joseph. "Pa's taking the wagon to the chapel. I'm taking my sisters home safely."

"Think I can sleep over?" Slainie pointed to her father, who was still serving spirits around a keg. Some men started clapping, and one of them sang an old Walloons favorite. When the adults started singing "We've moved to Canada with Marie Doudouye," the children knew their parents had gone daft and squinty. It'd be a long time before Mr. Lafont was ready to leave, and Slainie didn't want to stay without her friends.

"Of course you can stay over." Zoe locked arms with Slainie, and they strolled together out into the darkness.

CHAPTER TWELVE

Death Conquered

1861 / 10 years before the fire

THE MORNING AFTER the barn dance, Slainie woke to Marguerite tearing the room apart.

Slainie sat up. "What are you doing?"

"I'm looking for my veil."

"Is someone getting married?" Slainie asked before noticing the lace Marguerite pulled out was black. "I mean, did someone die?"

Marguerite headed toward the stairs, stopping in the doorway. "I want to wear my new veil to the chapel today. We're all downstairs—waiting on you actually. Get up, so we can go."

Slainie wanted to know more about the man who had threatened Adele's parents, but she waited to ask about it so as not to cause Mrs. Allard any concern. After eating a mushroom omelette, she joined Joseph, Zoe and Marguerite outside.

All around, shrubs and grasses had sprung from the ground, coaxed by spring rains. The forest foliage seemed denser than it had been only a day ago. Slainie followed her friends to the trail. "So, is anyone worried about who's going to be at the chapel today?"

"Pa must be there still. He didn't come home last night."
Marguerite took inch-perfect steps around every puddle on the
trail.

Zoe pulled her shawl tight around her ears. "I fear for Adele
if that obscene man went there. What if he brought others along
too?"

"Stop worrying. Pa and Henri didn't go alone. There were
probably a dozen men who went with them." Joseph smiled
slightly at Slainie, as if to reassure her. Maybe he noticed that she
still felt uncomfortable in the woods.

"When we get there, you will be staying, right?" Slainie realized she sounded much too enthusiastic. "I mean, we need someone to walk us home later."

"*Ouais.* Of course." Joseph nodded at Slainie as he slogged
through the muddy ruts in the trail. Marguerite and Zoe giggled
to each other.

Slainie had always thought of Joseph as a big brother, playful
and dependable—like her brothers should have been, but weren't.
Now, she noticed something in Joseph that wasn't there a year
ago. True, he had always been protective toward girls. He was
good-natured that way. But this was something else. He concen-
trated on her eyes when they spoke, at least more than she had
ever noticed before. He paid extra attention to her, as if he wanted
her to notice *him*. And she did.

When they arrived at the clearing, Slainie was impressed by
how many people were at the chapel. The crowd from a year ago
was puny in comparison.

Marguerite pulled the veil over her hair. "So much for some
quiet prayer time." Then she hurried into the chapel.

At the entrance, Slainie read the inscription her father had
told her about: "Our Lady of Good Help, pray for us." Inside,
at the end of the center aisle, sat a surprisingly ornate table. Two

women in black bonnets stood beside it, singing, and a glass lantern hung overhead. It looked as if a hundred people could fit on the benches Slainie's father had crafted. A pattern of brown tiles covered the walls and ceiling, but nothing lined the ground to soften it for kneeling.

Eight crutches leaned against the wall next to the altar. Baffled by their meaning, Slainie studied them. The armpit supports were carved at a curve in order to cradle the user's body comfortably. The crutches had been used so much that the wooden hand grips had worn down to a gloss. In an instant, Slainie was struck by the weight of importance this chapel had for so many people. *Eight crutches. Eight miracles. Eight pilgrims who travelled here for help and left crutches behind because their visit had healed them.*

Back outside, Slainie spotted Adele by the beloved trees and Mr. Lafont in the crowd, singing softly. *He looks so serene, like a young man.* She slid in next to him. When he finally noticed her, he pulled her in for a hug.

"Was that *man* here when you arrived?" She blurted into his ear.

"What man?"

"The one who hollered at Adele's parents at the dance."

"Oh, that one." Mr. Lafont looked like he hadn't slept all night. "He wasn't here when *I* got here, but I had forgotten all about him. I've been listening to different preachers all morning."

Mr. Lafont put his finger to his lips and then pointed to Adele who was responding to an emotional man in the crowd.

" . . . God is with you, and God is with her."

Hearing Adele's sincere tone, Slainie's chest felt warm. The image of Mary that had hung in the old chapel—the one with her heart on fire—flashed through her mind.

The man pleaded with Adele. "What should I do? What am I supposed to give her, to say to her, to help her out of this?"

The man's wife, a sickly woman, leaned into him with all of her weight, barely standing on her own two feet.

Adele spoke calmly. "Go to God together. God truly is nearer to you than ever before. He bears this pain with you."

The wife wept into the man's shoulder. "That doesn't help! She won't eat. She hasn't spoken a word since—"

Parting the crowd, Adele approached them. "Maybe I can offer some comfort. I tell you as I understand it. This young lady who has died was too young to gravely sin in the eyes of God. She wasn't able yet to make well-reasoned decisions about her actions, about good and evil. She wasn't yet seven, was she?"

The disturbed man closed his eyes and rested his face on the side of his wife's head. After a few silent moments, he managed to compose himself. "Our daughter was sixteen. Something was wrong with her. She argued over everything. She would not come with us to the church. She did not act like other girls."

Adele settled a hand on the weeping woman's back. "You cannot judge the state of a soul. You cannot assume a person's home for all eternity. You may see the outside appearance of a person, like the cover of a book. But only God can read that book correctly."

Slainie thought about "a soul," not knowing quite what it was. It wasn't something that came up during the lessons she'd heard at Marie's house. She thought of her sister Cecilia. *Did God give her soul a home for all eternity?*

The man hugged his wife closer, consequently pulling her away from Adele's hand. "What comfort does that give us? Not being able to know. Worse—knowing what we do know about our daughter?"

"Let me try to explain better. There are circumstances to every man's life that only God sees, and He doesn't only see it through His justice. He is perfectly just and perfectly merciful. So imagine a man does something horrible—he flew into a rage against his son, and you saw it. You would think, 'What a wicked man.' All the while, God knows that this man used to belittle and harass a very many people in his life every single day, and that this was the first time he had lost control of himself in many months."

Stunned, Slainie looked to her father for a response. *He is still a cruel man, even if it is only once in a while.*

Adele continued against a murmuring that arose in the crowd. "When God sees your sins and decides to show you mercy, I believe these circumstances matter to Him. If the abusive man is using all his strength, all his will, to stop doing this sinful thing, his sin would look different to God than to us. Sometimes, change doesn't come all at once. It comes slowly as habits change and virtues grow. The man is working with God to become better; he's just not there yet. He's practicing a new way to live. He can confess and receive God's grace to help him continue that change."

"I always thought our daughter was sick," the man said, as if thinking aloud. "She did not act like other girls. If she were sick, then maybe her rebellion against us could not be helped."

"My dear friends, listen. Whether it be a repentant sinner, a child, or an incompetent person, we can never be certain someone is in heaven unless they are declared a saint by Mother Church. That being said, if you are wondering about your sick child, it is not foolish to *hope* she is in heaven. Continue to pray for your daughter, that her dear soul will go to Our Loving Father."

Suddenly, Mr. Lafont touched Slainie on the shoulder, his eyes full of tears. "It's okay, Slainie." He spoke softly in her ear. "Your sister is in heaven. It's okay to be happy."

Slainie stood dumbstruck, unsure what he meant. She turned to Adele, who was at least ten feet away. She thought of charging over to ask her where else Cecilia could possibly be. Then, something clicked. *She was only four. I understand. She was just four.*

As tears fell from her eyes, she felt something deep and formerly impenetrable break open. A gigantic pressure lifted from her chest. She realized her sister wasn't gone. It was good to hope, good to believe she was somewhere better. It was like Cecilia had been raised from the dead—in Slainie's heart.

On the walk home, Pa broke the sleepy silence between them. He put his arm around her. "You're cold. This breeze doesn't feel like summer air, does it?"

Shivering, Slainie rubbed her arms for warmth. "It's the sun setting that makes things so cold." She leaned into him.

"You seem thoughtful," Pa said. "And you haven't heard the real good news yet."

"What's that?"

"The saints can see us from heaven. We can talk to them and they can help us. Why wouldn't Cecilia do that?"

Slainie's head hurt. Too many questions drowned out her brain's ability to respond. *If Cecilia is with God in heaven, what is heaven like? Does it rain? She loved playing in the rain. Is she still four? Will she be four forever?*

"I don't mean to make your head spin. I've thought a bit about this already. If Cecilia is in heaven, she is with God. If you tell her your problems, she can take them to Him. She's closer to Him, right? And that's what saints do, so you should talk to her. You can even pick flowers for her. All those things like you used to do. We can't let her life go by without some gesture. She is not gone. She is still your sister."

For several weeks, Slainie couldn't stop thinking about what her father had told her. At first, she felt like she was walking around with an invisible friend, like Cecilia was sitting at the foot of her bed or peeking over the table's edge while she ate. That feeling soon went away, but when Cecilia's birthday arrived,

Slainie knew her sister would want a celebration. Cecilia would have never missed the chance to go to a party.

The evening of Cecilia's birthday, Mr. and Mrs. Lafont were going shopping in Bay Settlement. Mrs. Lafont never marked the date in any special way, so Slainie asked Mrs. Allard to bake her a rhubarb pie—a secret pie. When Mr. Allard arrived to pick up her parents, Slainie snuck it off the back of the wagon before her mother came out to leave.

Once her parents were gone, Slainie went to the sewing basket to fashion some decorations. At the dinner table, Modette helped her cut strips from cloth and empty sugar bags for braiding into garlands. "How do you think Mother will respond to this whole thing?"

Slainie untangled some thread. "I don't know. But she has to have thoughts or feelings about Cecilia, and I want her to talk about it. Don't you?"

Modette stopped cutting and looked up. "It is not the place for me to speak. I never knew our sister. I was merely a baby when she died."

"You would miss her if you had known her. Maybe this will work. Maybe Mother will stop carrying her memories in silence. Then we can all enjoy our Cecilia together."

When they'd finished the braided garlands, the girls pinned two yellow ones to the ceiling above the table. The longer one dropped so low it touched the table's surface. Plates, cups and the pie sat on one side of the garland. On the other, Slainie had arranged some white and purple wildflowers—ones Cecilia would've liked. Then she lit three lanterns to brighten the kitchen.

Slainie hung the last garland over the door outside. "Now Mother will expect something. She can't be upset if she's given fair warning, right?"

For a long time, Slainie sat, anxiously watching out the

window. When she couldn't bear the wait, she began to tidy the house. Then Modette fashioned Slainie's hair into a large display of braids and ribbons, but Slainie grew tired and decided to lie down in her bed.

The sound of wagon wheels riding over gravel woke her. Leaping to her feet, she yanked the ribbons and braids out of her hair. She was flattening it with her palms when her mother entered the cabin carrying two buckets full of barley grains. She tried to set her things on the table, and after rattling the plates, she looked up at the garlands but said nothing. Modette offered to bring in the rest of the groceries. Then Mrs. Lafont turned to the sink.

Slainie sat at the table. "Maman, I did this for you."

Mrs. Lafont plucked potatoes from a bag to scrub them clean.

"Maman?"

With her potatoes bobbing in the water, Mrs. Lafont placed her hands at the edge of the basin.

"It's Cecilia's thirteenth birthday." Slainie's voice came out forceful and firm.

Finally, Mrs. Lafont turned to face her. She looked like a rag wrung out, with her eyes all squinted and lips pursed. She was angry, very angry, but she came to the table and sat down.

"How does this honor her?"

Modette came in with a large bag of flour. Seeing them sitting there, she dropped the bag and walked back outside.

"I talked to Papa. He told me Cecilia can see us. Adele said she is still with us because she is in heaven. She can speak to God for—"

"This nonsense still, Slainie? It's been more than a year since I told you these things were not true. You've been listening to your father tell fables. He told me this also, but there's no magic that keeps us alive when we are dead," said Mrs. Lafont.

"It's not magic, Maman. It's true. Cecilia was so good. She

was good enough to be with God. She was so young. Don't you believe it's so? Don't you want to?"

Her mother was yelling now. "No, I don't. I don't believe she is anywhere but in that grove in Kaukauna where we buried her. That's where she is, where she has been for eight years. You want to have a birthday party? You can go there!"

Slainie spit words out through her tears. "Can't we tell stories about her? Can't we be happy to talk about her? Why are you so hard . . . like a hard . . . cruel . . . *beast?*"

Slainie cowered, anticipating a slap. When it didn't come, she looked up at Mrs. Lafont, who sat, staring across the room. All she did was blink . . . blink . . . blink, like a clock keeping time.

Still staring. Still blinking, she said, "I am going to bed. Take this mess down."

That was it. Mrs. Lafont left Slainie crying alone at the table.

CHAPTER THIRTEEN

The Wars

1861 / 10 years before the fire

AFTER CECILIA'S BIRTHDAY, Slainie's sadness gloomed over everything like spring's overcast skies. She was weary of the wars all around her—the war with her mother and Adele's war against disbelief and the slander of her name. In April 1861, America began tearing itself apart when an actual war started: The Civil War.

At the kitchen table, Slainie bent over the most recent copy of *Frank Leslie's Illustrated Newspaper*. There, on the cover, she inspected a war scene: men who had formed a human chain were handing cannonballs from one to the next. At the end of the chain, gunners loaded cannons with gunpowder and soldiers dropped the cannonballs inside. Then they packed the concoction with a rammer. In the image, balls of smoke and fire flew above the walls of their fortification.

Mr. Lafont strutted past the window outside, startling Slainie. His voice boomed confidently as if he were making a speech. "Hundreds of men—even boys—all from the settlement. All Belgians."

From the bench on the porch, Slainie's mother joined in. "They're happy to fight, Jacques. They each get a sign-up bonus— the one we'll get too, if you go for us."

Slainie's father continued his speech. "And, son, think of all this country has given us. Think of the future you have here. We are Americans now. You already know what the North is fighting for."

The Civil War touched home for Slainie that afternoon. A few days later, her brother rode off to fight.

A week after Jacques deployed, Mr. Lafont hustled into the kitchen. He reached out to set something on the table, but seeing Slainie there, furtively shoved *the something* into his rucksack.

"Slainie! What are you doing home?"

"Is there somewhere else I should be, Papa?"

Her father sat next to her. He laid his bag on the table and out fell the silver tin that held his straight razor.

She picked it up. "Where are you going?"

Without warning, her father called for Modette and Vincent to come sit beside Slainie at the table.

"I'm going with Jacques."

Slainie grabbed Modette's arm. "You're almost sixty, Papa!"

"And, you're almost eighteen. What's that matter?" Pa took a deep breath. "Listen, we need the second bonus to grow our farm. We need to buy more cattle and hogs."

Vincent lurched toward him. "Then I should go."

"No. Stop now. I know the money doesn't matter to you, and it's not the whole truth. The whole truth is that I can't have one of my boys off fighting by himself."

Tears filled Slainie's eyes. Her father wiped one from the tabletop and placed his hand on hers. "I'll convince Mother to allow you to go to the chapel whenever you want. Will that bring you consolation while I am gone?"

She didn't think so, but she nodded anyway.

With Mr. Lafont gone, Slainie and her siblings had to carry the load of their father's labor and farming jobs. Everyone in the settlement took on the work of those off fighting. In a way, it made things easier, because Slainie and her mother hadn't the time to be upset with each other. They worked, went to bed and rose again to work until sunset.

When autumn came, so did a brief reprieve for Slainie. For three days, she helped Marie and her mother with the annual canning of tomatoes and berries.

At her kitchen counter, Marie smiled and chattered. "It was almost difficult to return home. In two weeks, I will start assisting Pauline LaPlante at the Holy Cross school house, and there is still so much preparation." She smiled at Mrs. Martin. "Yet I could not leave Mama in the lurch. The bushes won't clear *themselves* of gooseberries and strawberries, will they?"

Slainie forced a chuckle despite her dark mood. "I think the blackberries *did* pick themselves, seeing that the ground was purple underneath the bushes."

"I saw it too. We were a smidge tardy with the blackberry bushes. They are further away and always at the end of our rounds." Slainie wasn't going to fool her best friend with false laughter, and it really wasn't her personality to make quips. Marie's smile flattened. "What is wrong, Slainie?"

"What? Nothing is wrong with me." She let a spoonful of jam drip slowly back into the pot, as if inspecting its thickness.

"Is it your papa being gone?" Marie cleaned one of last year's dirty jam jars, handing another to Slainie.

Slainie would lose all control of her emotions if she went down this road. Maybe she could convince Marie it was only the war. "Yes. I do miss Papa."

"Are you still allowed to visit Adele while he is away?"

"Yes. I have been." Recalling her last few visits to the chapel, she teared up. She had sat off behind the crowd, listening to Adele and trying to take everything into a heart that was slowly freezing over, like Lake Superior in wintertime. To stop her tears, she started babbling.

"I guess I am still interested in seeing Adele, but I am alone nowadays. I do not feel much there. Zoe is with you in Green Bay. Marguerite? She is always inside the chapel, always praying. I would not want to bother her. She is discerning whether she wants to be a consecrated sister or not. I usually go when Mother will not ask me about it, usually when I know Mother is not going to need me. I might stop, though. I am not finding it as enjoyable as I did before."

"Did you hear something you do not like? It is not the doubters, is it? You do not doubt Adele's story, do you?"

"I've heard the attacks on her. It is nothing. I just do not want to go anymore." Sluggishly, Slainie added her fifth clean jar to the twelve Marie had already completed.

Marie wiped her hands on her apron and pulled Slainie away from the sink. Walking out of the parlor, they passed the china and bisque dolls on a shelf covered with dust. "You wouldn't want to take our friends down for a play, would you?"

Slainie's eyes widened with a flicker of joy, gone in an instant. "No, I would be no good at making believe today."

On the porch, Marie took some ruffled chair cushions and placed them on two chairs. Sitting, she took Slainie by the shoulders and looked her in the eyes. "Tell me."

Compelled now to be vulnerable, Slainie revealed how awful her mother had been, how badly she had tried to bring Cecilia back, and how much sadness weighed on her. As she wept, Marie hugged her. After several hours had passed, Slainie was smiling and feeling foolish about behaving so pitifully.

Venting to Marie cleared Slainie's mind. She decided to

continue going to the chapel and, as Marie had suggested, learn how to find a purpose in her suffering. That meant she would need to approach Adele and ask to talk privately, for Slainie had no idea how suffering could be anything more than pain. Invigorated by this new question and full again with curiosity, Slainie hiked to the chapel whenever she could.

Just as her bitterness was fading, Mrs. Lafont began coming to the chapel too, and always with her sewing baskets. She found work among the pilgrims, though Slainie was sure most of the women could have done such mending themselves had they packed any sewing supplies for their pilgrimage. Before long, Mrs. Lafont brought ready-made shirts and pants. It riled Slainie to see her there. She had hoped so many times that her mother would come to the chapel. When she finally did, it was only to sell clothes. For over a year, Mrs. Lafont had ignored every chance to accompany her. She really had no interest until her husband and son went to war, and they needed more money.

Slainie resumed avoiding her mother. Then, one night before bed, Mrs. Lafont suggested bringing Mr. Lafont's alcohol to the chapel. She had kept his tiny brewery going while he was away.

Under the lean-to behind the house, Slainie stared at a barrel full of fermenting liquor in the flickering light from the lantern in her mother's hand. She hesitated until she thought of a non-argumentative way to oppose the suggestion. "What made you consider this idea?"

"Well, I know a man from the bay sells his tobacco there, and that Breuger boy sells his father's cider. Why shouldn't we do the same?"

"I don't know. Alcohol? At the chapel? I mean, it is a place of prayer. The Virgin Mary touched earth there. It is holy. Sacred."

"People also nap in the shade there. They change their clothing there, eat meals, and meet friends there. Moreover, it isn't a sin to have a drink." The light shook in Mrs. Lafont's hand as she became more upset.

It wasn't a sin, but that wasn't the point. The chapel had become a market place, a circus. The bishop still threatened to remove Adele from the Church because she couldn't always maintain control of people on the chapel grounds. Slainie remembered a story from one of Marie's lessons with Adele. Jesus Christ had come into the temple—God's holy house—with a whip and turned over all of the money changers' tables. *If only someone would do the same at Adele's chapel.*

She looked at her mother and spoke calmly. "I saw a drunk man attack Adele's parents once. He said there are people in the church who want the chapel torn down. They say Adele is lying. And, I have since learned why."

"Why?" demanded Mrs. Lafont. "Well? Tell me."

"Because of this. Because of people—"

"Just say it . . . people like me."

"Maman, I understand why you are going to the chapel, but now so many come only to make money off the pilgrims there."

"Am I not a good person? I don't do this for myself, girl. I have taken care of you and your siblings. I have worked until my fingers bled."

"I know, Maman."

"Then, it's settled. Tonight, we will bottle a dozen pints. Tomorrow, we will bring them to sell."

Slainie glowered at her mother. "I really don't want to."

"This isn't a choice. Your father is off fighting. The bonus is spent. I can't sew enough to make the money we need, and Christ knows you can barely sew to bring in a centime."

"I *am* trying, but I will not do this with you."

"Then, I will do it myself." Her mother stormed inside, flung open a cabinet and tore through glass pint bottles. She had to yell over her own clanking and slamming. "You have always been ungrateful. Who do you think you are, standing in front of me like you have some higher view, like you are better than I am?"

The next day, Mrs. Lafont sat on a wooden box with a pint in one hand and a dozen more in a bin next to her. Slainie could hardly look. She lost faith in some hidden goodness inside her mother. She lost hope that she herself could resist growing into the callous person her mother was. She now believed what had been true all along, that as she listened more and more to Adele she walked toward Mary—and walked away from her earthly mother. Mrs. Lafont wasn't walking with her. As Slainie stood near the sacred trees, she let anger and pride encase her heart. She clung to the idea that she was right, and Mrs. Lafont was wrong.

For two months, Mrs. Lafont didn't speak to Slainie. She only sent commands and instructions through Modette. Finally, Slainie's father received a furlough and returned home for ten days. He was malnourished, with sunken cheeks and deeper lines on his face. His once square and muscular frame was frail and bony. After a few days of hearty meals, he was strengthened and happily filled the house with conversation and laughter again. He lifted everyone's spirits, but then only briefly.

The war wasn't done touching their lives. When Congress passed the Conscription Act, Jacques had to continue fighting and Vincent needed to enlist. The act forced all men between the ages of twenty and forty-five to join the fighting. Fortunately, Slainie's father was past the cut off and the commanding officer of his regiment discharged him. Slainie and her family received word that Henri, Joseph and their brothers wouldn't have to go to war either, because the Allards could afford to pay for replacements.

A week later, Mr. and Mrs. Allard came for tea and shared some terrible news—Joseph had decided to enlist after all. As his parents explained, he didn't think it right to send someone in his place.

With a distant look in her eyes, Mrs. Allard slowly stirred her tea with a spoon. "He tells us he couldn't handle wondering for the rest of his life if someone had died instead of him."

In the spring of 1863, at the age of nineteen, Joseph went to war. Slainie felt sick to her stomach whenever she thought of him. Almost daily, headaches and fatigue afflicted her and put her in a state of unshakable irritability. She blamed Mrs. Lafont for her sickness. She blamed her mother's hostility, as well as her constant presence at the chapel, the only place Slainie could escape her troubles. She simply couldn't continue working in the home alongside her mother. There was only one place she could think to go, a place where she'd be welcomed with open arms. Slainie decided to ask Mrs. Allard if she could stay in her house, in Zoe and Marguerite's room. If anyone could convince Slainie's mother of anything, it was sweet Mrs. Allard. The two women were so different, but Mrs. Lafont regarded her as a good friend. To Slainie's surprise, Mrs. Lafont agreed some time apart would be best for both of them.

Slainie would have never left home without her mother's permission. She never wanted to hurt her mother or be disobedient, but she didn't want to argue with her or be ignored by her either. On her eighteenth birthday, Slainie's family had a small celebration. Avoiding any conversation, Mrs. Lafont cleaned and gathered all of Slainie's things from around the house.

At the table, Slainie's father swallowed a large bite of prune pie. "Your mother's going to miss you."

"Why doesn't *she* tell me that?" Slainie turned to Modette. "I wish you would come with me."

"I don't need to leave, Slay. This is something *you* need to do. I'm okay right here, doing what I've been doing."

Slainie rolled her eyes. "You should be going to school now." Modette smiled and laid her head on Slainie's shoulder. "We're going to miss you, sister."

After pie, Slainie brought her bags out to the porch and waited for the wagon. She wanted her mother to come outside and say something. She wanted to see her cry, to see any display of emotion from her. She wished for a hug or an apology, but she didn't get either. Finally, she heard the wagon rumble off in the woods. She couldn't bear it any longer, so she opened the door where her mother was washing up in the kitchen. Coming from behind, Slainie threw her arms about her mother's waist. Mrs. Lafont stood stiffly.

Then, for the first time in Slainie's life, she told someone "I will pray for you," and she left.

Lying in bed on the first night away from her mother, Slainie imagined seeing Mary on the trail in the woods. Drifting off to sleep, she filled her mind with a white light, like sunshine through fog. She imagined the hazy outline of a woman appearing and drifting among the trees. Long, blonde hair floated about her head like dandelion fluff. When the woman turned away, Slainie ran down the trail after her until she fell asleep.

CHAPTER FOURTEEN

Finally, A Teacher

1864 / 7 years before the fire

MRS. ALLARD SET a pair of slippers on the bed next to Slainie. "These are for you." Slainie recognized them as Mrs. Lafont's work and slid her feet inside their wool lining. She thought of her siblings crowding around the stove in her family's kitchen. For more than a year, she had been living with the Allards. Now, she felt the pinch of guilt because she didn't miss home at all. Life at the Allards' was comfortable, much more so than life had been in her family's drafty little cabin. It was also quiet. Of the Allard children, Henri remained the only one at home.

Slainie wasn't expected to do any work, however, and she had grown unbearably bored months ago. After asking if she could help around the house, Mrs. Allard began teaching her to cook. She taught Slainie all of her tricks, like soaking carrot slices in cold water to help them cook faster and how to use up every last crumb of stale bread in delicious ways. One day, while they were in the kitchen, Mrs. Allard asked if Slainie wanted to go to school.

"Yes, but isn't this more important?"

Mrs. Allard pushed her roller across a thin circle of dough.

"School is as important as all of our knowledge about farm and home. It may even be more important . . . as things change."

"What is going to change?" Slainie patted smaller balls of dough into circles next to Mrs. Allard.

"You have seen that giant contraption out in our field, yes? A steam-powered engine is exciting to many, but there is a new engine that can operate on the liquid in that lamp next to you— kerosene. It comes right out of the ground. The ways we farm are always improving. God has gifted man with such a wonderful mind, and education helps it to reach its full potential."

Slainie beamed at the mention of God in ordinary conversation. She was getting used to the way religion permeated all parts of life in the Allard home. After a moment's thought, she returned to Mrs. Allard's original question. "I don't know if I would be any good at school."

"How about we start simple. I know just the person to teach you. It won't be penmanship and arithmetic, but it certainly will feed your soul. I will see to speaking with your mother about it."

The next day, Mrs. Allard came into Slainie's room waving a letter in the air. Unable to contain her smile, she sat down, unfolded the dirty page, and read it aloud:

> Ma Chère, *Slainie. I have been gone many months now. I think about home very much. I am grateful for the comforts I have there. This time in my life is trying my strength but know that my spirits are not dampened. I will not write to you of the devastation around me. I only want to tell you that, when I think of all I left back home, I have thought of you above all else. This was surprising to me at first, but now I understand. I hope you will still be in the*

settlement when I return. I wish to see you. Please
pray to Our Lady of Good Help for me.

                                                  Joseph

After Mrs. Allard finished reading these words, her eyes shot
up to Slainie's face. "Oh! I had a feeling this was so."

Slainie looked back blankly.

"You had no idea, did you?"

"What?" asked Slainie.

"Miss Slainie Lafont, our Joseph may be in love with you."

Slainie looked down at the letter and recalled the last few
times she had seen Joseph. The dance. The walk to the chapel and
the snickers from Zoe and Marguerite.

Slainie's eyes widened. Mrs. Lafont laughed. "My goodness,
I have said too much."

A week later, another equally surprising event was in store. In
the silent house, Slainie waited for her teacher to arrive, anxiously
bouncing her feet under the dining table. Suddenly, Mrs. Allard
bounded down the stairs. "She is here!" Slainie shot up to follow
her to the door. Mrs. Allard swung the door open, and Slainie's
jaw dropped. She was face to face with Adele Brise.

After the initial shock faded, Slainie smirked at the cleverness
of Mrs. Allard. *I can't believe it. She managed to achieve what I
wanted all along.*

Adele walked over with a tender smile and cupped Slainie's
face. "I finally get to teach you."

Mrs. Allard ascended the stairs. "I will be up here if you have
need of anything."

They sat, and Adele prayed in French from a leather-bound
book. Her words were soft and steady, having the rhythm of a
well-loved song. In that first prayer, with her eyes closed, Slainie

forgot all about the horrible injury Adele wore on her face. From afar, Adele's height and stern authority had convinced Slainie that she would be intimidating to talk to in a more personal setting, such as Mrs. Allard's dining table. Slainie never did summon the courage to approach her at the chapel. Yet, here she was, and Slainie found her manner no more imposing than a child's.

Their first lesson was how to make the sign of the cross.

"On that holy day, in the woods, Our Lady commanded that I teach this to you." Taking hold of Slainie's fingers, Adele tapped them on her forehead, on her chest and then across her shoulders. "In the name of the Father . . . and of the Son . . . and of the Holy Ghost. This sign is used very often in our faith. Every prayer you utter should commence and finish with this sign. It wards off evil."

During some of her lessons, Mrs. Allard read for them from the Bible, such as the day Adele taught Slainie about the office of the pope. She read the book of Matthew where Jesus Christ gave the "Keys of the Kingdom" to his disciple Peter and made him the first leader of the church—the first pope. Slainie could imagine a line of two hundred men stretching all the way back to Jesus, all linked by their service as leader of the Roman Catholic Church.

Finally, Adele taught Slainie about the life of the Virgin Mary as the Bible recorded it — the prophecies about Mary, her betrothal to Joseph, her choice to carry Jesus in her womb, the first Christmas, losing Jesus in Jerusalem, the miracles she witnessed, her presence at the foot of Jesus's cross, the descent of the Holy Spirit, and her life with the apostles, spreading the messages of her Son.

"I heard you had no idea who she was, I mean, when you saw her." Slainie spread gooseberry jam on a waffle, took a bite, and sat back to listen.

"I did *not* know. She never told me. The first two times I saw her, she only hovered, bright as the sun. I was so frightened, I fell to the ground."

After wiping her mouth with a napkin, Slainie put her waffle on its plate. Meeting like this for several weeks had finally put her at ease with Adele, so she let her questions spill out one after the other.

"Did you not tell anyone what you saw?"

"My parents and my priest. He is the one who gave me the courage to speak, to ask the lady who she was."

In excitement, Slainie pressed both of her hands flat on the table. "What did she say? What did she say *exactly*? I would like to know her very words."

Adele's eye slowly rose to the ceiling, as if calling the beautiful lady to mind. "'I am the Queen of Heaven, who prays for the conversion of sinners.'"

Slainie nodded, her eyes locked on Adele.

"She told me to pray for nine days, to make a confession, and to receive the Eucharist for the conversion of sinners. Then she commanded me to teach the children of these wild woods—to teach *you*—what is necessary for salvation in Jesus Christ."

Slainie gasped. "Was Jesus there, too?"

"I'm sure He was, because the Virgin began to fade out of view, and as she went, she turned to someone and asked for a blessing on my three companions."

"You saw Jesus?"

Adele shook her head solemnly. "No, that was not Our Lord's will. I could not see Him, but He would be the only one from whom Mother Mary would request a blessing. Who else could she have been addressing when she turned to ask?"

Slainie had seen almost nothing of religious art, but she knew Jesus was called the King of All Creation. She gazed long across the cabin, staring into space, and daydreamed. She saw the shining shape of a man on a throne and Mary resplendent in crown and mantle next to Him. It struck her how astonished Adele must have been.

"After that, I fainted." Adele closed her prayer book and began to rub it with an oil cloth. As she did so, she closed her eyes and smiled warmly, as if she had been complimented. "You must know already that I remember you. I know this isn't your home. I met you and your mother the day I came to your door. Two autumns ago, if my memory serves me well."

Slainie's gaze fell hard to the table. "I am sorry my mother was so rude to you." Flushing red, she recalled that afternoon when her life changed course while she sewed unsuspectingly by the fire.

"I miss my mother. Then I don't miss her . . . but then . . . I think I should."

Adele put a hand on Slainie's. "You miss your mother, as you should. You miss her as she is, but you also miss everything she was not."

Slainie wiped tears from her cheeks.

"The only perfect mother is Our Lady, Our Mother Mary: the Most Pure, Most Admirable, Most Kind Mother. You must reach for her when you feel this sadness. She will reveal to you the peace that comes from her Son. She will hear you if you pray about your mother, and she will show you how to love your mother in spite of all your resentment and pain."

Mrs. Allard's footsteps sounded upstairs. Lowering her voice, Slainie leaned closer to Adele. "There is something more that confuses me. I think my friend is in love with me. The trouble is, I am merely eighteen, and I think I cannot return his love. I still want to leave the settlement for an education."

Adele sat up, repositioning herself on the wooden stool. "Let me tell you a little about myself. On the day of my First Holy Communion, back in Belgium, all of us were there in our white dresses. We were simply giddy with love for God. Together, my friends and I made a promise to Mother Mary that we would become missionaries and serve poor children."

"So, your calling was clear to you."

"No, it was not. Do I serve the poor *now*? The Lord called me away to America. I begged Him to let me stay and fulfill my promise, but my confessor told me to obey my parents' wishes, so I went. Now, look what wisdom is in the Lord, what righteous labor he had planned for me here."

Adele stood and tied her book for the walk home. At the door, she took Slainie's hand. "You must pray every day, all the time. Ask Mary's Son to reveal your path."

She straightened, gesturing with her hands passionately. "What I can say for certain is that you are ready for your First Holy Communion. We're through with our lessons, but please come to the chapel to see me from time to time."

Slainie leapt. "Oh, thank you! Thank you!"

"Once I get word to Father Daems, I will be able to tell you exactly when you can come to Green Bay to confess and receive the sacraments."

Striding down the front walk, she turned back to Slainie. "Oh, I forgot to tell you—they call me *Sister* Adele, now."

A few weeks later, Slainie was in the kitchen, trying to salvage an egg mash she had overcooked. Out the window, a dark figure stepped off a wagon. *Why, it's Adele.* But the woman wearing the black habit and bonnet turned out to be Marguerite.

When she arrived at the door, everyone crowded around her. Henri tugged on the side of her bonnet, giving her a funny look. It had been altered by stitching a wide length of black fabric around the bottom that fell over her shoulders like a religious sister's veil. Mrs. Allard swung at the bottom of her habit with a rag, trying to clear off the dirt.

A few hours later, Zoe arrived. They spent the entire night talking and giggling in their room like they always had. Slainie tried to return Marguerite's bed. Refusing to take it, Marguerite threw a blanket and a pillow on the ground instead.

Zoe started unpacking, laying her items across the foot of her bed. She giggled. "You look just like Sister Adele now."

"Good," said Marguerite, "because I am going to be her translator when she travels into towns seeking money to build a school."

Zoe handed Slainie a pamphlet that had the drawing of a peasant girl on it. The girl knelt in front of a lady with roses on her feet.

"That is for you. She is Bernadette Soubirous, a French girl." Zoe pointed to the image. "Here is the Virgin Mary as she appeared to Bernadette."

Zoe handed Marguerite a jar with liquid inside. "Thousands of people are visiting France to see this chapel. In that jar is water from the miraculous spring."

Slainie admired the image of Our Lady on the pamphlet. "Thank you. Did you go there?"

"No, no." Zoe chuckled. "One day, Xavier Martin took me to meet a French couple from Canada. They had been to Lourdes and had souvenirs with them. They kept calling Adele's chapel the 'Lourdes of Wisconsin.'"

Marguerite removed several boxes of dolls and beads from under her bed. "Should Adele build her school, the students will make good use of these." She dumped them into a bag full of old books and trinkets.

Zoe cocked her head, brow crinkled. "You are leaving *now*?"

"Soon." Marguerite turned down the flame in her oil lamp and lay down. "There's a glow on the horizon. It's almost morning, and I am exhausted. Goodnight."

That afternoon, Slainie and Zoe woke to Marguerite gently shaking them. "I have something to show you."

Slainie looked at Zoe, whose eyes were half-closed with sleep. Zoe shrugged. The girls left thinking they were going to the chapel, but Marguerite took them to a small farmhouse next to an empty sheep pen. As they approached, a woman in an apron was leaving a small basket on the stoop.

Marguerite opened the door, and inside they saw Sister Adele. Plumes of dirt hovered around her feet as she swept. Slainie surveyed the room—a few chairs, some floor beds made of straw and quilts, and a carved wooden picture of the Holy Family on a small table.

Zoe and Slainie stood in the corner, trying not to hinder the transformation happening under Adele's broom. Slainie picked up the small basket, which was full of scraps from someone's winter cupboard, and Adele swept under it.

"Come. Sit." Adele leaned her broom against the bare pine wall.

The four of them talked until dusk spread another glow across the horizon.

Zoe and Slainie learned that the house belonged to Sister Adele. Several other women were coming to live with her there. All would don the modified black habit and bonnet. All would become third order Franciscans—like nuns, but with a different set of vows that would permit them to continue their work in the world, instead of the convent. Their mission was to teach the children who would attend their school, a school that was still only a dream in Adele's mind.

That night, Slainie and Zoe said "goodbye" to Marguerite, who had become *Sister* Maggie and joined Adele's mission for good.

CHAPTER FIFTEEN

Carrying Crosses

1865 / 6 years before the fire

SLAINIE'S EMOTIONS RANGED from joy to anxiety to disappointment as her First Communion approached. She wasn't sure she wanted it to come yet. The timing was all wrong. The Civil War had just ended and the Union had won, which sparked celebrations across the settlement as soldiers returned to their families. But then, President Lincoln was assassinated.

The Allards, however, were grieving for yet another reason: Joseph had not returned from the war. Of course, everyone had worried about Joseph's fate while he had been off fighting. Now that familiar worry turned into choking despair, especially for Mrs. Allard. She lingered about the windows while doing housework. None of the rooms had that orderly appearance that had been her signature, and she began to speak in monotone. Suddenly, Slainie found herself feeling like an outsider. While everyone worried and waited, she wasn't sure she should make her First Communion, considering all of the ceremony and gaiety that went along with the event. Should she celebrate if Joseph wasn't coming?

There was another person she hoped would come who probably wouldn't show up—her mother. Slainie had sent her an invitation. It even had a wax seal; but Mrs. Lafont never replied.

In spite of everything, at least Slainie felt ready when the day
arrived. If the problems in her life were unresolved, there was no
better way to face them than by uniting herself more fully to Jesus.
In a borrowed veil and white communion dress that used to be
Marguerite's, she strolled down the aisle of Holy Cross Church.
As parishioners bustled to their pews, she stepped softly in and
out of long colorful rectangles of light cast on the floor by the
sun. She surveyed the pine ceiling that hovered high above her
like the forest it once was. Then, she found her place in a pew
next to Adele.

As she smoothed the ruffles of her dress to sit, she noticed
her father and Modette smiling heartily from the other side of
Adele. Suddenly, a hand pulled on her shoulder, and she turned
to see Henri—and all of the Allards—smiling at her from the
row behind. Even Marguerite and Zoe had come. All this attention made Slainie want to leap out of her seat. She had to close
her eyes and calm herself with a few deep breaths. As Mass com-
menced, her thoughts wandered to Joseph. Each time she thought
of him, she wound the edge of her dress around her fingers. She
also couldn't help but repeatedly glance over her shoulder at the
doors, hoping her mother would surprise everyone by showing
up. Each time Adele noticed this, she crossed herself solemnly,
and it redirected Slainie back to the Mass.

The moment finally came for Slainie to eat the Body
and Blood of Jesus for the first time. She hardly believed it
was real, that she was walking toward the sanctuary. She still
felt like a fledgling, as lost as she had been four years ago, the
night she slept in the woods. She knelt before the altar, as
Father Daems gazed out across the row of children. One by

one, each opened their mouths to receive what only looked like bread.

As Slainie waited, she imagined she was hosting a ball, and Jesus was her guest of honor. Her soul was a palace that needed to be decorated for the King. What sacrifices could she set like golden platters on the tables? What deeds could she hang like tapestries across the walls? What devotions could hold the flowers like crystal vases?

In the Eucharist, He will pour His life into me, she told herself as she waited to feel a piece of communion bread on her tongue. With eyes still closed, she heard the priest say, "Corpus Domini Nostri Iesu Christi custodiat animam tuam in vitam aeternam." He repeated it as he moved down the line of first communicants. He announced the blessed proclamation over and over, echoing in her ears. "Corpus Domini . . . The Body of Our Lord . . ." And the voice grew louder in her head. All the noise of babies babbling and parishioners whispering behind her vanished. She had gone far away from everything. "The BODY . . . of . . . OUR LORD," she heard again. This time it sounded as if the voice were coming from inside her. "The Body of Christ," the Voice asserted. It was forceful, but sweet. It echoed, the words swirling around themselves, drowning out her other senses. With no other words, it said, as though implanting the knowledge inside her heart, "See. Here. This *is* truly My Body, which I gave up for you, and this is *Me* becoming part of you."

At that moment, Fr. Daems placed the wafer on her tongue. There at the rail, Slainie was entirely filled with peace and weightlessness.

Sadly, the other children stood to leave the rail, ripping Slainie out of this rapture. Her eyes snapped open. She scrambled back to her seat, feeling disoriented and yearning to return to that place where she had just been, the place where

Jesus spoke so clearly to her. Later, Slainie told her father and
Modette all about her experience as they sat in the grass near
the church.

Spring came. Luckily, the Allards had work to fill their time
and distract themselves from worrying about Joseph. The farm
came fully alive. For a while, Slainie was up to her elbows in wet
garden dirt as she planted tomatoes and squash. After planting,
she was daily covered in hay and saliva, having fed spring chickens and birthed baby lambs with Henri in the barn. May and
June rolled by with no word about Joseph. Finally, in July, as the
scorching midday sun shone down on the fields, a messenger from
the Union Army rode up, his boots in stirrups on a study brown
horse. He handed Mr. Allard a letter.

A toothy smile spread across his face. "Says he's alive!"

Mrs. Allard read the letter aloud. Joseph had been injured in
Pennsylvania and lost his memory. He was sent back to Wisconsin because someone noticed his uniform, which identified him
as a member of Wisconsin's Iron Brigade. A medical train took
him to Harvey Hospital in Madison. Eventually, his memory
returned, and he asked for his father.

Mr. Allard immediately left for the hospital. After three
more weeks passed with no word, Mrs. Allard began to look
sickly again. One afternoon, Slainie found her with her hands
bobbing in the wash basin while she stared out the window,
motionless for what seemed five minutes. Slainie came up next
to her.

Mrs. Allard removed her pruned hands from the water and
dried them on her blouse. Her eyes remained fixed on the trail
outside. "Why have they not returned? I was planning the feast
for his homecoming, but maybe he has died while we have been
waiting here."

That night, Henri brought a basket of bread and a request for prayers to Adele and the other sisters. Then they continued to wait.

The following Saturday, Slainie stood tippy-toed next to the bean trellis trying to pluck high-hanging pods. Hearing someone yell her name in the woods, she turned to see Mr. Allard's wagon clattering down the trail. "Get Emilie!" he hollered.

Mrs. Allard was already racing from the cabin door. The wagon had to stop abruptly to avoid hitting her. Climbing up, she disappeared under the cover. Then, hand covering her mouth, she staggered back toward the house.

Mr. Allard's head popped out of the wagon, and he caught sight of Slainie again. "Go prepare the bed in our room."

Slainie ran upstairs to gather Joseph's things—his blankets and pillows, his books, even the old wooden figurines that lined his window sill. She rushed them to Mrs. Allard's room and drew back the bed sheets. After she retreated to her own room, Mr. Allard and Mr. Martin shuffled past the door with Joseph in their arms.

For days, Slainie thought about visiting him—what she might say and what she might see. Every time she climbed the stairs, passing his room on the way to her own, her stomach tightened. Was he in love with her? How would she respond to whatever state he was in? The doctor came. Zoe and Marguerite came. Neighbors visited with food. All day long, Mrs. Allard went in and out of his room.

On day twelve, Mrs. Allard handed Slainie a plate of waffles. "It's time you two spoke."

When Slainie entered, Joseph was sitting with one leg on a pillow. His eyes trailed Slainie as she took the chair next to the bed. That's when she noticed his shirt tied in a knot where his left arm should have been. She gasped, but immediately composed herself.

"I know, it's strange, isn't it?"

She tried to smile.

"How are you?" he asked.

"I'm okay. Your family has been very good to me."

"I heard you were able to make your First Communion." Joseph's voice softened. "I wish I had been there."

He shifted his hips a little, biting his lip and inhaling hard. Along with a missing arm, one of his legs was in a wooden splint.

"It's broken . . . in three places."

Slainie's eyes fell to his leg, but she quickly turned in her chair and stared out at the clouds beyond the window.

"It's okay. You can look," he said. "Did you get my letter?"

"*Oui.* Thank you."

"I hope it didn't cause you any concern."

"No. I liked it."

"I never sent it, you know." He smiled.

Slainie's breath caught in her throat. "Wait. That letter was not from you?" To her surprise, she was filled with sadness. Then, she realized that the letter was signed "Joseph," and she was quite confused.

"Yes, of course it was. I just never got around to sending it. It was in my knapsack when I was injured, but I never had my knapsack in the hospital. Someone in the brigade must have found it and sent it to the settlement. When I awoke, I didn't remember that I had even written it, until everything came back to me."

He caught Slainie's eye and they gazed at each other for a moment. Despite his injuries, his caramel brown eyes still smiled. He needed more than just the sponge baths he'd been receiving. His hair was greasy and he smelled like he had just come in from baling hay, but he was still such a handsome boy. Now, a man. She realized her head was pounding, and she averted her eyes.

"I know this is overwhelming," he said, "but I could use a friend to talk to."

Slainie inched her chair closer to the bedside. "I am your friend."

Her hand lay on the edge of the bed, and he slid his underneath it. "When I was lying in the hospital trying to remember who I was, I kept getting this image of a girl. She always had a basket of clothing. Over and over, I saw this girl. I told the doctor about it, and he told me to keep calling it to mind—that it could help me to remember."

It couldn't be. Slainie blushed.

His eyes fixed on hers again. "When the memory became clear, it was you, Slay, when you used to come to the house every week with our mending. You're the strongest memory I had."

Slainie lowered her head and little whimpers escaped her throat.

"I am going to come out of this, and when I do, can we go for a walk?" he asked. "Together, just the two of us?"

"*Oui,*" she muttered. "I . . . can't—"

Then she stood and bolted from the room. She flung herself down on her bed and wept. Eventually, she fell asleep in a mess of wet hair. When she awoke, she threw on her shoes. She didn't even notice the sun setting as she ran to Adele's farmhouse. Thrusting the door open, she spotted the sister at her table with a quill in her hand.

Adele's head jolted upright. "What's wrong?"

"I need to know why. I need to understand why God would send Mary to us, and then He would hurt us!" Slainie still stood in the doorway.

"Hurt you? God has not hurt you." Adele walked over with a lantern and closed the door behind her.

"I heard the Belgians gave more men to the war than any other settlement in Wisconsin. Explain this, Sister. Please explain why Joseph lost his arm when he had already made the sacrifice to go to war." Slainie squeezed Adele's hands. "I need to understand why we give our lives to God if it doesn't make life easier."

Adele led Slainie away from the door. "Come pray with me. Let's pray the Lord will help you understand."

"Understand what?" Slainie refused to move any further.

"Understand the purpose of the cross. Jesus had a cross, why shouldn't you? His cross was heavy, just like yours. He carried his cross, just like you must. His cross led to His death, just like yours will."

"Joseph's injuries are a cross? But Joseph does not deserve a cross, and I do not deserve a friend I cannot help. I'm still struggling with a mother who does not love me. A dead sister. I'm still struggling to take care of—to deal with myself."

"Jesus did not deserve a cross either. He is God. He is pure Love and Goodness." Adele relaxed into her chair, but her face became firm. "Saint Paul had a cross, did he not? A 'thorn in his side' he called it. He said the Lord would not remove it from him. Saint Teresa of Avila also. She had fits of anxiety. Saint Juliana of Liege was cast out of her monastery. The first Christians to follow our Lord? The martyrs of the early church? They accepted their crosses with gladness, celebrating Mass in hiding, knowing death was the risk they were taking. Without their crosses, these holy friends would never have become saints. Do you see? He commands us to carry our crosses if we want to grow. We cannot run from them or allow ourselves to despair of them."

With her face in her hands, Slainie rubbed the stress out of her forehead. "I thought my cross was my mother. I thought Cecilia . . ."

"And regard how the pain you felt pushed you to seek the truth. You would have been too satisfied with your life to seek God if you had not felt all of this pain. Everyone has crosses. All you can do is lift yours, the cross you have today, lift it high without a grumble. And when it gets too heavy, ask Jesus to come under and bear it with you."

Wiping her nose on her sleeve, Slainie had calmed down enough to sit in one of the wicker chairs. "Your cross, Sister— how do you carry it?"

"My eye, you mean? I lost my eye as a young girl, but I had already offered my life to Christ. I remember being scared, but if God saw fit to remove my eye, that was His right. He gives us everything, and He can take everything away, as He sees necessary."

"But, I have seen you in the snow. I have seen you in the dark, out in the woods. Why would God make the mission He had for you even more difficult?"

"To bring me to heaven. You see, all that matters is that we get to heaven and bring others with us. Suffering humbles us. It makes us need God more. Without that need, I may try to do it alone, and truly be alone."

After their talk, Slainie didn't feel better. Adele's words hadn't made Joseph's injuries any easier to handle. Not knowing how to help Joseph, Slainie felt powerless and frustrated. Likewise, the Eucharist had not erased any of her anger toward her mother. She wanted to feel closer to God, but she only felt defeated. All of her efforts to be a good person, to be "Godly," hadn't really changed anything in her life. Not as far as she could tell. She was ungrateful, and she knew it.

Fortunately, whenever Slainie visited Joseph, he mad

forget he had any injuries at all. He told her about all of the towns he had seen, not the battles he fought in them, but the buildings, the churches, the smells, the people, and the cuisine. With Slainie's arm to steady himself, Joseph stood for the first time. Again and again, he tried to walk with a cane. Finally, after four months, he hobbled away from the bed and out of the room.

Christmas came to Wisconsin, and with it, a grand party. All of the soldiers from Aux Premier Belges, including their families, packed the Allard house wall to wall.

Candles glowed in the bellies of winter squash and scrap-cloth garlands hung across the windows. Each time a new person marched into the house, he stopped in the doorway to stomp snow off his shoes. As the door swung ajar, Slainie felt the chill of winter air and inhaled the scent of pine. She maneuvered through the house replenishing platters of warm sugar cookies and passing out plates of braided bread with colorful vegetable dips.

The illness Mrs. Allard had experienced during Joseph's absence continued to riddle her body, so Slainie's mother came to help in the kitchen. Many times, Slainie was within arm's reach of Mrs. Lafont, although she never said more than "hello" to her daughter the entire night.

Slainie reached to take a plate from Zoe when the door creaked open and Sister Adele walked in. As Slainie headed over to greet her, Joseph started to speak from the living room. Somehow he had managed to stand on a chair without his cane. Slainie whipped around and pushed through the crowd toward him, afraid he might fall. As she reached his side, he began to speak.

"Friends and neighbors, thank you for coming. Thank you

to my parents for having all of us here. I would like to tell you something about my time in the war."

The room grew so quiet you could hear the stove crackling.

"I was shot on my first day at Gettysburg. This first bullet went into my arm. When we were pushed back, all of our soldiers tried to run to the ridge, but I could not keep up. My arm was bleeding badly, and I fell. That is when another soldier's horse trampled my leg. I watched the trees above me, smelled the smoke of muskets, and waited to die. Eventually, I passed out."

Joseph stopped speaking, but Slainie could hear him breathing heavily.

"I woke up in a mansion that had been converted into a hospital. I wanted to die. The pain was unbearable, and my arm was gone. Then, one day, there was a priest doing his rounds, and he gave me a rosary. I was so frustrated when I couldn't remember how to say it, but he taught me. Some days, I only managed two or three Hail Marys, but whenever I feared how my life would look as a cripple, Mary was there. I really felt her with me, and I promised her I would fight to get home."

Joseph lifted his hand toward Adele. "For introducing me to Our Lady, and for arming me with the best weapon I had in the fight, I want to thank Sister Adele."

Everyone clapped, and Adele lowered her head until they had finished. When Slainie looked back up, Joseph was climbing off the chair. With a hand on his cane, he stood before her. Mrs. Allard started hushing everyone, and the room fell silent.

"I made this for you, Slainie Lisette Lafont." Joseph held out a carved wooden ring. "I made this in the hospital while I waited to come back to you. I know it's not a real ring, but with it, I ask you to become my wife. I'll buy you a better one soon, I promise."

Dumbstruck, Slainie could only utter a soft "yes." She put

out a finger on which he could place her delicate ring. Joseph dropped down into the chair and pulled her onto his lap. Squeezing him around the neck, she whispered in his ear, "Any ring or no ring at all—I'm yours forever."

CHAPTER SIXTEEN

Final Warnings

SIX YEARS LATER

1871 / weeks before the fire

SLAINIE AND HER five-year-old daughter Odile were walking home after an exciting first day of school. Sister Adele's academy had been open for three years, and more than one-hundred students now attended. Most of them hadn't seen each other since last July, when their families had come to the school to watch them act out dramas on the last day of the year. How sad it was for Slainie to see the children cry and cling to one another as they parted for the summer. Now it was fall, and they were together again at last.

"It's too hot now, Mama." Odile tossed her wool cardigan on the trail and ran ahead. "Mama, guess what Lena said. Lena said Adele is old and mean. Do *we* think that Sister Adele is old and mean?"

Laughing to herself, Slainie bent to retrieve Odile's sweater.

"Darling, she is not old and mean, but she may be old and tired. Sister Adele has not been teaching children in the school all this time. She used to walk to their homes, through these woods. Remember?"

"Like us. Right down this path." Odile spun around twice, nearly crashing through a bush on the trailside.

"Careful!" Slainie lurched forward, but Odile stabilized herself. "Not down the trail we are on right now. Through the woods before there were any real trails."

"But she is not mean?" Odile asked again.

"No. You knew her before she was your teacher, Odile, and she has not been mean at all."

When they reached home, Joseph was pulling carrots from the garden. Slainie's one-year-old daughter Sophie sat in a wooden crate next to him. When she saw Slainie, she rocked and waved a stick in the air. Odile lifted her out and whirled her in circles. The drought had deprived the ground of anything to drink, so the children easily kicked up dust when they played outside. Both children were already covered in it. Slainie didn't even notice dirt anymore.

"Hey, Bucket." Joseph nodded to Odile, using his nickname for her. "Tell me of things at school."

Because of Joseph's injuries, Odile always followed him around the house, carrying his tools while he worked. That is how she earned her nickname. With only one arm and a permanent limp, he rarely accomplished his tasks alone. It pained Slainie to watch him struggle, but she smiled when she heard that sweet nickname—Bucket—because it reminded her that Joseph's injuries had strengthened the bond he had with their daughter instead of hindering it.

Odile put a carrot in Joseph's satchel. "Oh, Papa. William was hiding the plum tarts in his bed."

"Plum tarts, say you? That sounds messy."

"The tarts were smashed under his pillow. Sister Annie made

him bring his own wash—right away—to the laundry. Papa, he has to bake them all again . . . for everyone. *All* the tarts."

Raising an eyebrow, Joseph glanced at Slainie.

Slainie explained. "Odile is referring to the excitement at school yesterday. Sister Maggie had told the children that Sister Louise was baking tarts. When the tarts had cooled, Sister Louise brought them into the school room, but a handful of children did not get one. She could not figure out what happened to them. She was sure she had made enough for each child."

As Odile and Joseph continued their conversation, Slainie took the baby inside to finish supper. She latched a wooden gate that kept Sophie out of the kitchen and put some dough in the oven. Then she leaned in to taste the soup simmering on the stove. Filling the house with warm promises all day long, it smelled of rosemary and pig fat. As she watched the steam rise, she glimpsed a wagon coming down the road. It could have been her mother, who liked to visit in the evening to give Odile sewing lessons. Picking up Sophie, Slainie went outside. The wagon stopped in a cloud of dust, and Xavier Martin stepped down from the bench.

"Good afternoon," he said, as he went around to help his sister Marie get down.

As soon as she set foot on the ground, Marie bent to pin up the back of her skirt. She was getting ready to play with Odile and Sophie. Slainie rushed across the yard to greet her. Since Marie was teaching at the school in Green Bay, Slainie's dear friend didn't often come to call.

"Guess what, sweet Odile?" Marie knelt in front of the girls. "There are five of us at the convent now."

"Do you have to share your room?" Odile asked. "That is not favorable for you."

Marie laughed. "No, I still have my own room, but I would

love to share it with someone. It is so quiet after dark, and I do like to talk to someone when it is dark."

Shaking Joseph's hand, Xavier inspected the orderly rows of mostly brown plants in the garden. He shook his head.

"We have just come from a visit with our friends in Sugar Bush. They have experienced several lesser fires this week. If we do not get a good spot of rain, it could be devastating. A surge of wind at the right moment in time could spread an inferno without hindrance."

Joseph looked alarmed. "Who has already left?"

"I know of several families."

Joseph dropped his glove in the dirt. "Then, we better do the same."

Surprised, Slainie hustled to where Joseph and Xavier were speaking by the wagon. Then she looked out into the yard to make sure her girls weren't listening.

"But Odile is in school now."

Joseph put a reassuring hand on her shoulder. "We can return home after the new year."

Xavier agreed. "Many of the people I have conversed with expect the cold weather to slow the frequency of these fires. Nevertheless, people are meeting at the chapel tonight to discuss whether it would be prudent to leave the region presently as a precaution. Better safe than sorry, as they say."

"We will come, too." Joseph turned to Slainie. "Would you pack supper for us?"

Nodding sadly, Slainie went inside. As she pulled jars from the shelf to fill with stew, she noticed smoke billowing out of the oven door. Panicked, she hollered for Joseph, who hobbled inside. He threw the oven door open and lifted the smoldering loaf with a rag, tossing it into the wash basin with a splash.

Slainie hugged him. "I am sorry. I am really sorry."

They looked out the window together.

"My pa will give us a wagon if we decide to leave," he said.

"How can you decide in such haste that we should go? It is not that easy for me."

He turned her shoulders so she faced him.

"Listen, I can take some burnt bread from the oven. That I can do . . . but I have only one arm, Slay, and a lame leg. If the big fire comes, we are going to need a head start on it."

When they arrived at the chapel that evening, it was standing-room only. Slainie brought Odile next door to play with the other children in the school room. On her way back outside, she popped into the kitchen where Sister Louise hefted a large bag onto the table. Fresh loaves of bread rolled out along with various roots, cabbage cores, potatoes, and spotted crab apples.

"Adele's midnight vigils to Our Lady always produce abundantly. We will have a lovely vegetable soup and some kind of apple bread pudding. I can manage that. Let us see—there is some syrup somewhere around here." Sister Louise poked her head inside the pantry.

Slainie told Sister Louise about the fires in Sugar Bush and then she went to the chapel. As candles and lanterns flickered against the chapel walls, Adele addressed the settlers from the altar. Slainie could see the long black sleeves of her habit raised over the crowd, but could not hear her above a rowdy tiff between several people who disagreed on the frequency of the fires and the level of urgency to leave. Slainie had never seen a crowd so riled up.

Standing in the back, Slainie suddenly heard her name. "Slainie? Slainie? I cannot find Odile!"

She peered out across the yard. Sister Addie emerged from the darkness, panting as if she had been running up and down the stairs.

"We were in the school room. I was reading. When I turned the page, she was gone."

Handing baby Sophie over, Slainie sprinted to the school room. She knelt on the ground for a look under the tables and benches. Odile wasn't there. In the kitchen, Sister Louise said she hadn't seen her. Slainie ran up the stairs and searched the girls' dorm. All the cots were neatly made. A rectangular box sat at the foot of each, where the children kept their belongings. One-by-one, Slainie flung the boxes open. She did the same in the boys' dorm across the hall, not finding Odile in any of them.

Slumping down on a cot, her mind conjured up the worst case scenario. *Odile has run off into the woods. She overheard us talking about the fires. She must be terrified. She has run off to find help or shelter.* Suddenly, Slainie remembered how scary the woods were at night when a girl was lost and alone.

Just as she had decided to get Joseph and form a search party, a soft voice came from under a nearby cot. She silently crept closer and heard Odile jumbling off a prayer.

"And, God, school just started. You can't take it away from me. Adele and Maggie and Sophie . . . and Gran and Papa . . . and Grammy and Uncle Henri . . . they can't all come too. So we have to stay. Okay? You make us stay, and you take away whatever they're afraid of."

Smiling, Slainie knelt beside the cot. Odile hadn't heard them talking about the fires. She had no idea what everyone was making such a fuss about.

Slainie peered beneath the cot. "We have been worried."

Odile's head rested in the nest made by her arms. Shrugging, she peeked at Slainie over her shoulder. Slainie lay down on her back and shimmied under. There was barely room for her chest to expand as she breathed.

"Darling, tell me."

Resting her face on her forearm, Odile gazed at Slainie. "God is going to let us stay."

"We will pray for that." Slainie touched Odile's arm.

"But Gran isn't even here. She's going to stay home and not come with us."

"No, no, *ma chèrie*. You know Gran," said Slainie, referring to her mother. "She doesn't come to the chapel, but she will be okay. Nothing is going to hurt us tonight."

Odile sniffled, and tears splattered the floor beneath her.

Slainie wiped droplets off her daughter's cheeks. "I am really sorry you are scared. How about this—we will stay, and if Papa decides we need to go, we can just hop in the wagon for an adventure."

The corners of Odile's mouth slowly turned up, and her eyes widened. "An adventure!"

That decided it. Joseph agreed they could stay. Without any distant friends or relatives, there wasn't a place to go anyway. Furthermore, none of the chapel sisters were leaving. The entire peninsula waited and watched.

Two weeks later, there still hadn't been any rain. The fire horns in neighboring settlements blew often, but the small blazes there never reached Aux Premier Belges.

Anticipation cloaked everyone like cold morning frost.

Slainie hated the tightness in her own gut, so she distracted herself with a last-minute project. With only two days before the big annual celebration, she decided that Odile needed a new dress.

CHAPTER SEVENTEEN

Fire

SLAINIE SAT AT the table shoving pins into the hem on Odile's new dress. The celebration at Adele's chapel was tomorrow. All morning, she had been snipping and sewing ferociously. The bun in her hair, held up by a knitting needle, kept falling strand-by-strand into her face. "I'll fix it," Odile announced, as she reached across Slainie's arms to stuff the hair back in. Slainie swatted her away.

"A little space would help me greatly. Could you go play with Sophie?"

"Mama, it has to be done today. The other girls have to see it."

"I know, Bucket."

"You can't call me that. Only Papa can."

Slainie laughed. "Guess what, *Ooo-dile*. Aunt Zoe is coming tomorrow, too."

Odile ran a circle around the room and landed with a thud next to her mother's feet. Dropping the dress on the table, Slainie pulled her daughter up off the floor.

"Remember, tomorrow is not about your dress. It is about the Virgin Mary and the day she visited Adele."

Odile bounded out of the room. Slainie took a deep breath and called after her.

"Come get your sister."

Once the girls had gone outside, Slainie could finally focus. While her fingers worked, she listened to Odile describe her dress to the baby, who grunted and tottered through the yard. When their voices trailed off, Slainie stood to listen more intently. Odile went around to the back of the house, but had Sophie followed along behind her?

In a moment, the girls were giggling with the goat Odile had lovingly named "Scratchy." Her worry appeased, Slainie sat back down to finish the final hem on the dress. Scratchy usually bleated whenever she heard the children outside. Lately, though, this signal that the girls were out back had become unreliable; the goat bellowed all the time.

Once Slainie had tied off her last stitch, she strolled outside, swaying the dress in front of her. Scratchy bleated at the sky with her four small hooves together on a stump. She looked as if she would topple over, but she had excellent balance. Wincing at the goat's shrieks, Slainie scanned the backyard. She presented Odile's dress, holding it out in front of her, but slowly lowered it when she spotted Sophie smeared all over with ashes.

Glancing up, Slainie noticed small ash mounds on the roof. Raining ash from nearby fires had become a familiar occurrence, along with the echo of fire bells sounding in nearby settlements. Odile liked to smush the gently-falling flakes between her fingers, drawing white and black streaks up and down her hands. As Slainie approached, Odile quickly turned away. Sophie continued to innocently grab at falling ashes with her chubby fingers.

Nothing about the scene alarmed Slainie, other than Odile's disobedience. "I told you not to play in the ash. I told you it could still be hot."

With her hands behind her back, Odile faced her mother.

"You can't see your new dress with hands like that. Now, go inside and wash up."

That night, Slainie and Joseph tucked the girls into their bed and told them a bedtime story, the one they retold in great detail every year. Like their beloved tales of knights and kings, Slainie told her girls about the queen who lived in heaven. She was queen because her Son was "King of the Whole World." And she loved everyone in the world so much, she gave her Son to them. Yet, they didn't care about her precious boy. They deserted him and beat him and killed him. But, one day, she visited—the queen came down to the world from her heavenly throne. See, her Son, the King, was alive and well again. The queen wanted to help the people repair what they had done, so she delivered a message to the Belgians of Wisconsin, a personal invitation to return to Him, her Son. He would forgive them. They only needed to follow Him again and tell others to do the same. Odile remembered this story.

"I'll wear my dress for the Prince, too," she said. Then, to Slainie's surprise, she rolled over and obediently went to sleep.

As she left their room, Slainie slid the brown window curtains closed. Tomorrow's celebration would have them all up late, and she wanted to prevent the morning sun from waking her daughters. Joseph had already gone to their room, where he was lighting another lantern. For several hours, they reminisced about their childhoods, which was always vividly on their minds as the anniversary of Adele's apparition approached.

Slainie sat cross-legged on the bed. "You remember how scared I used to be . . . of everything?"

"I remember, though I never knew it at the time. You seemed good-tempered to me, always curious and unaffected by much."

Joseph lay on his side, propped up on one elbow, hand supporting his head.

"Now you know better."

"Yes, you were quiet, which made you seem all right even when you weren't." Grinning at her, his eyes gleamed in the flickering light.

She grinned back. "I didn't like you."

Joseph rolled over and shot up. "Yes, you did. What does that mean?"

"I didn't like you more than I liked Henri or my own brothers. You were strong and helpful but—"

"I sure hope I still am." He relaxed back down onto his pillow, staring up at the ceiling.

"You are. I can't imagine how I didn't notice you sooner. All those years running around in the woods together. Sleepovers with Maggie and Zoe. Barn Dances. I was so caught up in my own head, in my own troubles."

"Until Adele came." Joseph turned off his lantern on the bedside table. Sliding under the quilt, he nestled his head on Slainie's crossed legs and kissed her knee.

Giggling, Slainie ran her hands through his stiff hair. "*Oui*. Until Adele came with all the answers I needed." Bending to kiss his cheek, she slipped her leg out from under him, lay down and closed her eyes.

Several hours later, something jarred Slainie awake. She jolted upright in her bed. Along with Scratchy's incessant braying, a cacophony of clucking, mooing, and squealing came from outdoors—the uproar was frightening. Slainie leapt out of bed and froze at the window. *Smoke!* The intensity of the red haze, like a sun setting in the middle of the forest, was proof enough that this fire was big enough to reach Aux Premier Belges.

After Slainie roused Joseph and the girls, they hurried to gather clothing and food. Then they fled to retrieve the rest of Joseph's family from his childhood cabin. Following her husband, Slainie sprinted along the edge of the wheat field separating her cabin from the Allards'. As she tugged Odile behind her, the five-year-old resisted. Her short legs couldn't keep up. Impeded by his war injuries, Joseph stumbled on a rock. Sophie cried out. With a grunt, he kept from falling and limped on, squeezing the baby in his good arm.

When they arrived, Mr. Allard was standing on the timber steps of his porch, pointing behind them toward the fire glow.

Joseph halted at the bottom of the steps and eyed his father. "Pa, come down. We're leaving."

"Mother has refused." Mr. Allard groaned and slammed his fist on the wooden post at the top of the railing. "I told her this one is bigger, that we would have to leave. Woman will not listen to me."

Joseph's brother Henri bolted from the house. "Fire looks about five, maybe as much as seven miles away. We would be lucky for an hour to get ahead of it."

Slainie placed Odile's hand in her uncle's. "Stay with Henri for me. I'm going to go get Grammy." Henri scooped Odile up in his arms. He gave her a tickle, growling like a bear, and gaped back at the woods.

Inside, Slainie didn't see Mrs. Allard in the kitchen. As her eyes bounced around the room, scanning for her mother-in-law, her gaze fell on the chair where Joseph had asked her to marry him. She remembered Mrs. Allard laying the table with pies and her heart ached. Soon, the fire would devour everything before her. Running upstairs, she poked her head through each door-way. Nobody. Anxiety vibrated in her gut, and she bounded back down the stairs. *We don't have time for this.*

Suddenly, a *creak* came from the corner of the house. "Mama?"

"I am here." Mrs. Allard's voice was weak and sullen.

Slainie discovered her mother-in-law in the reading nook that Mr. Allard had built for her. "Mama, why were you not answering? The fire is coming quickly."

"I guess I did not hear you." Mrs. Allard gently rocked in her chair, staring down at a book.

"Why are you so calm? We need to leave right now." Slainie's heart pounded.

"I know." She turned a page.

"Then, what are you doing? You need to come with us."

Mrs. Allard had never irritated Slainie before, but Slainie's blood raced through her veins. They needed to run! She wanted to grab her mother-in-law by the arm and drag her outside. "This one is bigger. People are fleeing in their wagons."

"I saw them." Mrs. Allard nodded to the window. "People have been leaving for weeks. It is only a brush fire, like it always is. It will go out, like it always does."

For the most part, Mrs. Allard was right. The drought had left things brittle and perfect for kindling fires. Every day, fires started when trains threw off sparks or farmers burned brush. Sometimes, piles of sawdust spontaneously ignited near a mill.

"I am certain it is more than a brush fire. Have you not seen the sky?" Slainie pointed at the orange haze out the window. "Please get up. You are wasting time."

"Slay, you go. I cannot go with you. Honestly, I will only put you all at risk if—"

"No, you will not." Slainie pulled hard on the frail woman's arm, surprising Mrs. Allard enough to let out a little gasp. Feeling ashamed, Slainie let go and stepped back.

Mrs. Allard cradled her arm and looked down at her body. "I will only slow you down."

"I have always respected you, Mama. You have been sick for a long time, and I have never questioned your strength. I have never pushed you to do anything. Today, though, you are not staying here."

With that, Slainie stormed outside. A moment later, she marched back in, Henri behind her. He cocked his head to the side and scowled at his mother.

"You know that you have to come, Mama, because if you refuse I will lift you over my shoulder and carry you out. You can kick and scream, but I will not let you stay behind. We have an hour to get in front of this."

Frowning, Mrs. Allard clutched the wooden rail on the wall next to her and used it to stand. "My children, you have no idea how difficult this will be for me and for all of you."

Slainie understood it was hard for her mother-in-law to be a burden to her family, especially while they fled for their lives. At least she didn't need much time to pack. She merely grabbed a loaf of bread, a jar of jam, and extra shoes for Henri on their way to the door.

When they stepped outside, the slim road through the settlement was jammed with wagons, a dozen or more inching by as slow as wheat grows. The expanding glow had pushed everyone out of the woods. All those horses and oxen, sheep and goats, neighed and brayed as they were squished against each other.

Henri had fetched a donkey and a goat. On the goat's back, he tied a small cage with four hens crammed inside. "The road's no good. I think we'd better go on foot."

Joseph smiled when his mother walked out onto the porch. "Mama, I think you should ride on Francis. It should spare you a bit."

Staggering over, Mrs. Allard ran her hand down the donkey's

back where its hair grew in a black cross. "How are we to get your sisters, Joseph?"

Joseph grimaced as Sophie, who wanted to get down, clawed at his arm. Then he gazed north above the illuminated trees. "They are safer than we are. Green Bay has a fire hose or two. If we have seen smoke, they have too."

"You forget. Maggie is at the chapel." Gathering up hand- fuls of her brown skirt, Mrs. Allard stepped close enough to the donkey that her hip rested on his flank. She was ready for help mounting the beast.

Over-tired and thoughtless, Odile wandered off toward the house. Before she had taken her third step, Slainie spun her back around. Slainie held her close while she looked to Joseph. "We should get Maggie from the chapel. The fire is driving us east anyway."

Mr. Allard must have been thinking the same thing. Holding his lantern up toward the trees, he put an abrupt end to everyone's considerations. "Ahead!" He nodded. "The trail is just there. Get a move on."

Without hesitation, Joseph, Slainie, and Mr. Allard darted toward the impenetrable-looking forest with Henri leading Mrs. Allard on the donkey.

Slainie struggled to see the trail in the bouncing light of Mr. Allard's lantern. To make matters worse, her panting five-year-old began to ask the questions she had feared. "Mama, why is Grammy on a donkey? Why can't we slow down for Pa's leg? Why is the night so bright? Why are we running? I want to eat. When can I eat?"

Trying to calm the little one, Slainie repeated over and over, "No need to worry. We are very close now." She glanced back, and instead of the warm glow from earlier, flames rippled through the branches. She didn't dare tell Odile that a fire was gaining on them. Without thinking, she tugged the girl's arm again, and her wailing intensified. Slainie dreaded the thought of having to carry Odile if she became too weak to run any further.

As they sprinted and stumbled through the dark, weakness spread down Slainie's legs. In her fatigue, she lost focus and caught a whiff of the crisp, lemony scent of Douglas fir trees. Her mind instantly latched onto the peaceful memories. She had smelled her first lemon when Mr. Bisset brought a crate of them from California. Her pace slowed. *Oh, that smell is like Christmas and Mrs. Allard's custard. And that one time Mother used a lemon to scrub the butcher block clean of berry stains, and it worked.*

Mother! The thought of her mother left all alone suddenly terrified her. Slainie's father would expect the settlers to converge on the chapel. If he was in a panic, he might run to the chapel in hopes of finding Slainie and Joseph there. Her mother, however, had only gone to the chapel when she could profit from it. Otherwise, she refused to go, no matter what the reason, no matter who invited her. Slainie didn't want to face this fire without her family or wonder how to locate them afterward. *We should be together. Let Mother be there. Let her follow Papa there.*

Lost in thought, Slainie slammed into the donkey's hind end. It was attempting to nibble the grass along the edge of the trail. Mrs. Allard let out a pitiful yelp. Henri tugged the rope and the beast scuttered ahead.

Spinning around, Mr. Allard sent the lantern light into a violent bouncing of shapes and shadows. Stunned, everyone froze as they lost view of the trail. Without a hint of fear, but with a dire tone, Mr. Allard scolded them all.

"Pick up your feet. Do not stop. Do not straggle. Keep those beasts in line."

Suddenly Joseph grabbed Slainie's arm. "I can't . . . " he struggled to say, and she thought of his limp. Because his left leg was shorter than the other one, he had to heave his body to the right with each step in order to keep pace. Dropping Odile's hand, she immediately took Sophie into her arms. The instant she had released Odile's hand, the little one clutched and tugged frantically at her mother's skirt. "Mama! Don't leave me." Grasping in the dark, Slainie connected Odile's hand with Joseph's and sprinted to catch up with Mr. Allard again.

Odile continued to plead that her mother stay with her. At the sound of her daughter's desperate voice, a wave of despair surged through her. The chapel became a horrible place for them to go. In vivid flashes, she imagined all of them perishing there beside Adele, Sister Maggie, and all the pilgrims. *Marguerite should have gone to New York,* she thought angrily. *She would be asleep in a room full of fabric trimmings and fashion sketches right now. Instead, she is in these woods—these God-forsaken woods—facing a God-forsaken fire.*

Mr. Allard was hefting Odile on his back when they turned off the trail and entered the chapel clearing. Then, in the light of so many lanterns and campfires, Slainie realized how hard Joseph had tried to keep up. His body seemed boneless as he collapsed against the fence. Henri helped Mrs. Allard slide carefully off the donkey's back. Mr. Allard flopped down next to Joseph, rocking a senselessly rambling Odile in his arms. In the steady motion of running, Sophie had fallen asleep. Slainie passed her limp body into Henri's hands.

"I will get everyone some water," she said.

She charged through huddled groups of people, hearing murmured prayers and plans to search for better safety. Some settlers argued about how far away the fire was and how quickly it would travel. Nearby, an old woman spoke thoughtfully. "There are not many trees in the clearing. The fire will most likely jump us. We are safe here." As Slainie hustled to the well, she scanned the faces of her neighbors and friends, the majority of whom waited with a look of stunned terror in their eyes.

Carrying a large tin of water, Slainie returned to find Odile trying to free herself from Mr. Allard's lap. She obviously wanted to run off and play, which is what she would have typically been allowed to do at the chapel, but her grandpa only held her more tightly.

Across the crowd, Slainie spotted her father. She waved vigorously. "Papa! Modette! Over here!"

As they hurried over, Slainie realized another fear had come to pass.

"Mother is not with you?"

Mr. Lafont shook his head regretfully. "You know she never comes to the chapel. I should not have left her, but I had to come. I had to see if you were here."

Slainie stomped her foot on the ground, half frustrated and half determined. "I'm going to get her. This time, she needs to come here."

Modette seized Slainie's arm. "What do you mean? You mustn't go out there."

Slainie whirled around to face her. "Do you not see what is happening? The fire is coming, but she will not come to the chapel on her own. She will not."

"I can go," Joseph interrupted, but then his gaze fell to the ground. He and Slaine both knew he wouldn't be able to run.

This is it. Finally, this is my chance. Now I can repair everything. All of Slainie's guilt about leaving home so long ago rushed to the surface.

"I will be okay."

Joseph struggled to his feet, ready to protest, but Slainie ignored him. She knelt in front of Odile. "I am going to get your grandma now. You are to stay here with the others. Be good.

Listen to Papa. I will be back." She kissed Odile's cheek. "I love you, *ma chérie*."

When Slainie stood again, her father was an inch from her face, staring in her eyes. "Listen, *you* are NOT going after her . . . I am."

Slainie looked to Joseph, as if he would bolster her decision. He wouldn't. "You cannot leave, Slay. What about Sophie and Odile? You might not make it back."

Defeated, she hugged her father, but barely had her arms around him before he was off weaving through people as he headed for the fence and the still-dark woods beyond.

Like a creeping mist, smoke wandered into the yard, then into the chapel. People pushed to get outside for fresh air. Among them, Slainie spotted Sister Maggie, but in that hectic dimness, it was impossible to get her attention.

Odile was at Slainie's feet. "Mama, the baby wants you."

"What?" Slainie yelled, still scanning the crowd in the chapel yard.

"Mama, she is not sleeping anymore."

Slainie looked to Henri and saw that he was bouncing and shushing the baby. As she bent down to scoop up Sophie, she caught sight of the side of the chapel. It radiated an orange glow.

It is here!

As Slainie tried to warn Joseph and the others, an immense whirring sound rose above her voice. The fire was blazing in the woods to the west. Odile covered her ears and peered up at Slainie with questions and terror in her wide eyes. *What am I supposed to tell her?*

Joseph huddled over them, as Slainie and Odile helplessly watched the woods. The fire glowed behind rows and rows of trees, but it was getting brighter, getting closer. Sparks shot from the tree tops. A new tree ignited from every spark, then another and another, and dozens more until tongues of fire jumped along at great speed. The whooshing sound grew louder as people began to weep and shriek. Joseph hugged Sophie, squishing her ear into his chest.

Still to the west, the front row of trees stood calmly as if nothing was wrong. When the fire reached them they ignited with energetic bursts of flame. The leaves and needles burned first, right before Slainie's eyes, so that the last thing she glimpsed of each tree was a black skeleton of branches. It flashed for an instant before each tree disappeared. Nearby barns and houses exploded into flames and burned to nothing in a matter of moments. Odile stood entranced by the fire as it swirled around itself, sucking the air into a thousand tiny tornadoes.

Mr. Allard pointed north, and Slainie looked across the crowd. Out past the opposite fence and into the vast crop fields, more flames approached. Soon, two sides of the chapel grounds would be locked in by fire. Odile's face contorted as she observed small, dark shapes racing across a field. Until that moment, the fire had been way out there, a problem for the trees. But now, Odile realized people were being swallowed up in it. Slainie felt dizzy. She went dumb, for she didn't know what any mother could say to her children during such a moment. She could only hold them close. Just touch them and kiss them. With a mother's instinct, Slainie wrapped Odile in her arms as the girl whimpered and watched the pines and cabins and barns explode into flames.

Soon the fire spread to the south side of the chapel. Now north, west, and south were ablaze. Intense heat blew Slainie and the others back away from the fence. They all looked east toward the last fire-free section of forest. *I hope there's still time for Papa and Mother to make it back inside before the fire encircles the whole fence. If this is it, we need to be together. I need to see my mother, to apologize, one last time.*

Suddenly Joseph darted away from Slainie. She hadn't even the time to call after him before he was lost to view among the throng. Relieved, she spotted him only moments later. Without a word, he dragged her and the girls over to a hole in the ground. Sitting in the grass next to it, he pushed Odile down inside and handed baby Sophie to her. Four other children already huddled there below the dirt.

"You stay!" he yelled. "Stay until I get you."

Odile did stay.

Slainie watched as Joseph covered the hole with a wet blanket. *What is he doing?* She fought the urge to pull the girls back out as Sophie's little hand grasped the dirt at the edge of the blanket. Over and over, the blanket rippled with movement underneath. Every part of her body twitched to jump in and protect them, but the hole wasn't big enough. When Odile peered out, barely peeking her eyes above ground, Slainie lurched toward them.

Joseph hugged her tightly. Over the firestorm, he hollered something again and again until Slainie finally made out what he had said. "It's the only thing we can do!"

Slainie scowled and turned away. Looking east, she scanned the field for her father on the only side of the chapel that the fire didn't threaten. There, men and women crawled under the fence, many dragging children behind them. One woman tore the back of her shirt as she slithered through the posts. One by one, they came. One by one, until Slainie saw her mother clenching her teeth as she struggled under. She was so covered in red scratches and dirt, Slainie barely recognized her. Freeing herself from Joseph's arms, she shoved her way to the fence.

"Where is Papa?" Slainie screamed. "Where is he?"

Mrs. Lafont collapsed and stared back at the forest. Shaking her, Slainie asked again.

"Mother! Where did Papa go?"

Mrs. Lafont didn't answer. She appeared to be in shock. Staring at the fence together, Slainie remembered the girls in the ground and jerked away, running to the hole to peek in. Sophie must have struggled mightily to free herself, because Odile had the baby's dirty legs pinned between her own. They had rested their bodies against the crumbling wall and fallen asleep. The four unknown children cuddled together next to them.

As the smoke thickened, Slainie caught sight of people lying down to get under it. She curled up next to the hole, and with the tips of her fingers, pushed the edges of the blanket into the dirt to secure it in place. *Good Jesus, please do not let smoke get into that hole.*

Slainie had no one to cling to now. She had no idea where Joseph or the rest of her family had gone. Unable to comfort even her children, she was alone in the crowd of frantic people. She stammered every prayer she had ever learned. *"Holy Mary, Mother of sinners . . . fled to thy intercession . . . seeking thy aid . . . O' remember that never was it known . . . Hallowed be thy name . . . beneath thy compassion . . . accept at thy hands . . . O, holy angel . . . cast me not off."* Eventually, she could only sob and repeat, *"Have mercy on us."*

Someone began chanting, and as more people joined in, Slainie recognized the words of the Hail Mary above the thundering of the fire. One after another, people started crawling on their knees around the yard. They lifted a three-foot statue of the Virgin Mary above their heads while they prayed the rosary together. Slainie joined the procession, doing her best to keep her interior eyes on Mary and her physical eyes away from the flames. Exhausted and unsteady, she lumbered into the person in front of her and bounced off the person behind her.

The settlers crawled around and around the yard, changing direction when smoke choked them. They finished one rosary, then another. Slainie lost count of how many they had said, but she made a prayer of every effort to lift her knees. Longing to be with her children, she offered Jesus every jarring thought of losing her babies, her husband, and her own life.

Swiping a rock from her shin, she realized she had gashed both knees wide open and was bleeding. She toppled down on her side and wormed out of the way. Eventually, the roar of the blazing fire overcame the shouting, and she clutched her ears against the piercing, whirring sound. *This is it. I am going to die here, without my children, without Joseph.* She resigned herself to the idea that she had done all she could do. She had no fight left.

She lay still, pushing her mind toward God as if reaching for sleep. In her foggy-headedness, peace replaced fear. Slowly, progressively, she sensed a calmness about her and the discordant noises of the fire grew faint. Her eyes shot open. Gazing upward, she saw a strange clearing in the smoke above. Something serenely drifted there. Straining to focus, she spotted many of them, white and black and floating like feathers to the ground. *Those are ashes.* All of her other senses numbed as she watched them glide, as harmless as snowflakes.

Sitting up, she looked around, bewildered. The smoke had cleared so that she could see the crowd again. The procession had stopped. In silent amazement, each person gaped at the fence— the fire raged beyond it, yet did not breach the chapel yard. Flames rose like towers on all sides, but were restrained by some invisible wall, sealing the settlers in a fortress. Slainie wasn't hot, nor was she thrashed about like the trees she had seen snapping earlier. Aside from the ashes that fell so beautifully, the air around her was still.

Something extraordinary was happening.

The procession began again. Slainie joined, this time filled with hope. *You're going to save us. Of course, you're going to save us.*

CHAPTER EIGHTEEN

Downpour

TWO WATER DROPLETS splattered on Slainie's shoulder. *What is that?* Before she could glance at the tiny wet spots on her dress, sheets of rain started pummeling her. The procession halted. The flames ceased. Heavy showers extinguished the fire as quickly as a gust of wind changes direction. Arms out and eyes closed, Slainie tilted her head back to drink the rain. The settlers around her were overcome by fits of laughter and praise while they soaked their weary bodies.

Relief swept over Slainie, and she remembered Odile and Sophie hidden in the hole. She crawled through the mud until she found it. Sophie came out sleepy-eyed but breathing deeply with lots of beige and rose in her cheeks. Odile, on the other hand, was pale and didn't wake when Slainie tried to move her. A married couple, disheveled and dripping, suddenly flopped down next to the hole. They hoisted out the four other children. Brushing aside the children's grimy, blond hair, the couple walked off kissing their foreheads vigorously. Odile slumped into the spot where the children had been.

In a panic, Slainie looked up with wide, pleading eyes, hoping someone nearby would help her. She spotted Joseph already sloshing over to the hole.

"She's unconscious. Help me get her out."

They heaved Odile out of the hole and laid her on the ground. Hovering over her chest, Slanie heard the little one wheeze. Several times, Odile's eyes shot open as she tried to focus, but then rolled around before closing hard again. Slainie told Odile to rest, but she immediately tried to stand. When her legs collapsed underneath her, she relented and rolled onto her side.

In the mud, Slainie rested next to her, pointing out across the yard. "Look, *ma chérie.*"

Everything around them—everyone—was drenched and dripping. They beheld wet hair, skirts covered in mud, goats drinking from puddles, and sheep shaking themselves dry.

"A miracle," Slainie murmured.

Families across the yard hugged and cried, a look of tired disbelief on their faces. Grazing animals casually wagged their tails as if they had never left their own barns. Slainie spotted Sister Adele and the other sisters praying under the sacred—and undamaged—trees. Slainie's mother appeared in the crowd carrying a handful of oatcakes. She plopped down next to the children.

"Someone was handing these out." She gave a few pieces to Odile and Sophie. After a few nibbles, Odile lurched forward in a coughing fit and spat them out. With a raspy, pained voice, she whined and cried. Slainie placed a hand on her back and noticed the sound of coughing all around them.

Ten feet away, Joseph leaned out over the wooden fence. "Look, Bucket. Come look at this."

Supporting Odile around the ribs, Slainie struggled toward him. She gasped at what they saw—and what they didn't see. Beyond the fence, there was nothing but charred remains, nothing but black bits of wood lying here and there—black stumps, black fallen trees, mounds of black ash and dirt. No forest. No barns. No buildings.

Even the backside of the fence was black where the fire had attempted to devour them all. Yet, for some reason, it had stopped. In fact, the chapel and all of the five acres inside the fence remained entirely untouched. Not one living thing had been harmed. After hours of marching with the Virgin Mary's statue and pleading for deliverance, their prayers had been answered affirmatively.

Slainie's mother joined them along the fence, seating Sophie on the ground where she happily played, oblivious to anything but the squish of mud in her hands. As Odile stared at the black earth, her lips began quivering, and she pounded on Slainie's leg.

"Mama, where is Grandpa Lafont? Is he in the kitchen? Did he go home? Go get him! Mama, go get him!"

Slainie and Joseph stood dazed by fatigue and the view of devastation before them.

Odile swung out to hit Slainie harder. "Why aren't you going?"

Slainie caught her arm. "Odile? What?"

"Grandpa! Grandpa!"

Slainie bent down. "Oh, poor little lamb." As she hugged Odile close, her eyes scanned the crowds wildly. *Is he even here? Did he never make it back?*

With panic across her face, she turned to Mrs. Lafont. "Mother?"

Taking Odile into her arms, Mrs. Lafont grinned and pointed to a group of people sitting on the ground. "He is over there."

Odile jumped down and ran to Mr. Lafont. She leapt onto his back, clearly choking him in her grasp. With indescribable relief, Slainie watched her mother amble over and put her arms around them both. Everyone Slainie loved was there—her children, Joseph, Maggie, Henri, the sisters, her father, Joseph's parents and many of their neighbors.

A few days later, after the shock had waned, the survivors held a meeting outside the schoolhouse. Dozens of them, wrapped in tattered coats and shawls, discussed how to make a home at the chapel, a home alongside everyone else who had nothing out in the nothing. Snow could start falling in early November, just a few weeks away. They couldn't sleep on the ground forever. They would need to build temporary shelters. Even before that, a few of them should trek toward the bay in search of warmer clothing and blankets. If there were no towns left along the way, Green Bay *had* to still be standing.

As the survivors tossed around ideas, Adele and the sisters bustled into the crowd. Everyone quieted when they saw Adele. After leading them in a prayer for protection and guidance, she immediately doled out the spaces in the dormitory. Slainie and her girls received one cot.

The men voted and were all in favor of relinquishing their spots inside the dormitory to the elderly and the very young. Because of Joseph's war injuries, Slainie tried to convince him to sleep on her cot with their girls.

Joseph pulled her out of the crowd and around the corner of the schoolhouse. "I think creature comforts should be given to those who are weak and need to recover. My war wounds have healed, even if poorly."

With big, soft eyes, Slainie pleaded with him, gently tilting her head. He refused indignantly. "No. I will join the men outside."

Sweeping aside the hair stuck to Slainie's cheek, he lowered his voice even further. "You don't understand. There is a lot of work ahead of us, a lot of labor that I will be unable to contribute to. You take the cot, Slay. Allow me to be of good use, because the opportunity for me to be of good use seldom arises."

In the coming days, local papers ran articles on Adele's chapel, one of them calling it an "emerald isle in a sea of ash." This attracted visitors who began to arrive in great numbers again. They brought with them stories of other survivors. There were stories of loss, too. One family had jumped into a well and survived, while others who did the same had perished. All the residents of Williamsonville had fled to an empty potato patch, hoping the fire would jump the spot where no trees stood as fuel for it. Yet all fifty-nine perished. Others survived by lying in water and still others by covering their heads with wet blankets. These suffered terrible burns. One girl had clutched onto the horns of a cow and floated beside it in a river all night long. A few had crouched behind hills or giant rocks as the fire roared overhead. Many lay in streams and covered themselves with wet mud.

Reading of the miracle at the chapel, a priest named Father Peter came to share his fire survival story. Taking a seat on the ground, Slainie joined the growing crowd. She awaited Father Peter's talk, jittering and squeezing Joseph's hand.

The priest glanced up at the trees where the Blessed Virgin had appeared and then looked out on his audience with bright eyes. "I am here today because our Good Lord felt it a necessity to preserve my life for His use. There is no other reason that I should have come through such a calamity as these fires, while so many more righteous men have perished in them." Father Peter ran a hand through his salt and pepper hair. "Yet here I am to relay to you my story, which I find to be as incredible as the one you yourselves have experienced in this holy place."

Father Peter was from Peshtigo, the town where the fire had first erupted. He described the hours leading to the fire. "My neighbors kept about their lives seemingly unconcerned, but I could not ignore the unavoidable signs that something was strange. The sky was a dark grey, and I sensed eeriness all about me."

Slainie thought back to that day and realized she had also been unconcerned. Her mind had been on the children and the task of finishing Odile's dress.

From his spot in the shade, Father Peter continued. "So, I dug a trench . . . six-feet deep. I buried the church's vestments and ornaments inside. When it was time to retrieve the Blessed Sacrament, I stumbled. I dropped the key to the tabernacle, and I couldn't get inside to remove the Host. With no other choice, I had to place the whole tabernacle on my wagon and flee with it.

"At this point, the air was no longer fit to breathe, full as it was of sand, dust, cinders, sparks, and smoke. It was almost impossible to keep my eyes open. I came out through the church gate and entered onto the road. All about me, vehicles were crashing, horses were neighing, chimneys were falling, and trees were uprooted. The wind whistled and roared. People were stricken dumb in the noise and terror. Many just froze."

Slainie wiped fast-falling tears from her cheeks, as did many of the settlers around her. Their own losses were still fresh. Sniffling, an elderly woman addressed Father Peter, "Where could you go?" Someone else's voice wavered as she spoke. "How in all of heaven did you make it out?"

"I did not expect I would," responded Father Peter. "I knew the river across town was my only hope. I simply needed to make it there. So I pushed through the chaos and arrived at the shore. I rolled the tabernacle into the water and went in behind it."

A tall man's voice boomed over the whispering in the crowd. "You saved a whole lot of people, I heard."

"That is true. Many people were standing in frozen terror on both sides of the river, so I climbed back out of the water and pushed them all in. For a moment, the sound of splashing crashed louder than the fire, but we were not safe yet. The flames darted over the river as they did over the land. It was only by beating the river constantly with our hands that we kept the flames at bay."

Father Peter continued relaying his story to the people, describing how he finally knew the danger had passed. "After five-and-a-half hours in the river, all the while flapping our arms, I noticed the air cooled down."

Slainie flashed a smile at Joseph. This was her favorite part of the story, the moment when she had been certain they were safe. "The rain," she whispered, waiting for Father Peter to tell his version of the miraculous downpour that extinguished the fire. Father Peter, however, wasn't able to end his testimony as Slainie thought he would.

"I dragged myself out of the water at three in the morning and was surrounded by bodies, both of the living and the dead."

Standing in front of the crowd at the chapel, Father Peter paused. His expression grew blank and tired. His eyes were still on the crowd, but he wasn't with them. It looked to Slainie as if he were watching these memories.

Finally coming back to himself, his countenance brightened. "Several days after the fire, I returned to Peshtigo—and to the river. I was helping the injured when a parishioner ran over. The youth came to me and said, 'Reverend, have you seen what has happened to the tabernacle?' We walked to the shoreline, and there I saw the tabernacle from my church, floating atop a log. Everything around it was blackened by the flames: logs, trunks, boxes . . . nothing had escaped. Yet, there bobbed the tabernacle intact in all its snowy whiteness. We pried the tabernacle open, and the Holy Sacrament was still in its golden ciborium. Water had not been able to force the cover open, and the violent vibrations of the wind and river had not even cracked the communion bread. Even the heat of the fire failed to melt the blue satin lining of the tabernacle."

Upon hearing this, a wave of goosebumps rose along Slainie's arms.

Father Peter closed his talk with an invitation. "I never look upon that holy tabernacle without feeling moved by a love and veneration grander than any I have ever felt before. It will sit on the altar at the new chapel in Marinette, which is already underway. As soon as reconstruction is complete, I will send word that you must come and see it there."

Slainie looked out at the yard where her girls were running with other children. She stood to wave them over. "Odile. Come. I have just heard something exciting."

Slainie told Odile a child's version of Father Peter's story. To excite her, she asked Odile to keep her ears open and report back as soon as she heard word that the Marinette chapel was ready to receive visitors. Visiting another settlement, especially one that would attract pilgrims like the chapel had, was something to look forward to. It didn't carry a vague future date either, like the day their new house would be completed or when she might cook a nice stew in her own kitchen again. This trip could happen much sooner than that.

A week had passed when a letter from Father Peter arrived for Adele. It wasn't word of the Marinette chapel's completion. It was only a thank you for hosting him. Yet, along with the letter, he had included a leaflet. As Slainie listened to Sister Maggie read it, she could barely breathe. It was a public statement about Adele—a message that went out to his parishioners and all the local settlements. It read:

> *Church authority has not yet spoken on the sub-*
> *ject of Adele and her apparitions, but I would say*
> *that if it lay within the power of any of my readers*

to visit the spot where the Virgin Mary appeared,
I earnestly counsel you to go. The chapel is yet in
its infancy, but it is the only one of its nature in
the United States. There, you can see and question
Adele, who is the heroine of a good work. I feel
assured that, like myself, all those who go thither
will return edified and happy at heart, if not con-
vinced of the reality of Our Lady's apparition.

Slainie imagined all the people who would read this letter, not just supporters, but the irreligious, the skeptics and those who had never heard of Adele at all. When the letter ended, she threw her arms around Joseph. Wanting to join the fun, Odile wedged herself in between them. "Why Mama? Why are we supposed to be celebrating?"

Slainie drew her into the embrace. "Because the Lord has caused a miracle, and now Adele can continue to tell her story. Just look at all the people around us!"

Odile scanned the crowd, but she didn't show any signs of comprehending this good news. Slainie knew, though, that their miracle couldn't be denied, and Adele's story couldn't be ridiculed and stifled by naysayers any longer. God had made His blessing of the chapel obvious, first through the fire and now on the word of this good reverend. Time would tell if it was obvious to the bishop.

CHAPTER NINETEEN

Aid and Blessings

IN THE FIRE, the Belgians had lost everything they had ever built, every row of crops they'd toiled to plant, every homestead where their children had grown. Hundreds upon hundreds— maybe thousands—of settlers had perished. The labors of eighteen years, every moment since they immigrated to America, felt like a waste. If Slainie allowed herself too much time to sit and think, she would slip into gloominess and frustration. So she looked to the future and stayed busy caring for livestock and serving food around the dormitory. By introducing Odile to the mother in the cot next to them, Slainie had nudged her daughter to stay busy, too.

The young mother had lost her husband. After arranging to reunite with him at the chapel, they had planned to continue south to Milwaukee, where her sister lived. But her husband had stayed behind to load the wagon and didn't flee their home soon enough. Now the frazzled mother raised three children alone: a two-month-old who always cried, a two-year-old who climbed everything, and a four-year-old whose favorite question for Odile was, "Can you take me outside?" Relishing the task, Odile sat them on the edge of her cot and drilled them on animal facts and numbers up to ten. Suddenly maturing into her role as "teacher," she paced in front of them, retelling stories she had heard at Adele's academy. When they squirmed and tired of "school," she led them in games of hide-and-seek. In this way, she kept the two older children busy so their mother could feed the baby and calm some of the crying that often filled the room.

The night Slainie had fled the fire, she dropped her sack of supplies on the trail. She and Joseph had no possessions, but they soon found out the most important thing anyone had was a farm animal. Collectively, the survivors had three cows, a dozen or more hens, four donkeys, a tiny flock of sheep and two goats. That meant milk, butter, and soon, cheese. On average, the hens laid eight eggs a day, and everyone received half an egg on rotation, except pregnant mothers, who were given one whole egg *every* day. A handful of whitetail deer had also survived inside the fence. After the fire, they lingered near the chapel, the only spot where vegetation still grew. Some of the men ventured out into the blackened earth to hunt them, but never returned with their prize.

One day, a mail carrier making the long trip through the burnt district dropped a bundle of newspapers off at the chapel. As Slainie strode to the makeshift chicken coop to check for eggs, she saw Mr. Hasselt run to shake the carrier's hand. "*Merci*, sir. Thank you."

The carrier pulled off his brown leather coat, lined at the collar with bear fur. "Your chapel here is on the front page, and there's a bit of information inside that I think'll assist you. Might be good to read what's happening everywhere, I'd think." He handed his coat to Mr. Hasselt. "Someone else ought to benefit from this. You'll pass it on? I have another."

Grabbing a newspaper, Slainie read that the former mayor of

Green Bay, Mr. Samuel Cressy, and his wife Elizabeth, were given charge of local relief efforts. A mile from the fire boundary line, Green Bay hadn't suffered any damage. Winter's brutal winds and subzero temperatures were coming, and Slainie feared what might befall little Sophie and Odile. They needed more food and more clothing. They needed soap and blankets, as well as wood for cooking and heat. Joseph said the men were itching to find work and to bring home the lumber necessary to rebuild the settlement. They couldn't accomplish what they felt duty-bound to do because they only had sluggardly donkeys. They had no horses or oxen and no wagons for hauling.

Later that day, while Slainie and her girls fed barley to the chickens, Sister Adele told them she was going to Green Bay. The city reportedly received an overabundance of donations, and Adele was asking Elizabeth Cressy for a share.

"Mama, are there any people out there?" asked Odile, looking beyond the chapel fence.

Slainie flicked her wrist, scattering grain across the ground for the chickens. "Of course there are. Someday we will go back to the bay, and you can see."

Odile tugged Slainie's arm. "I'm going with Aunt Maggie and Sister Adele tomorrow."

Slainie shook her head. "No, Odile. Not this time." Odile stomped twice on the ground.

Slainie sympathized with her daughter, but who knew what she might see out there in the burnt district? "Now stop. It is not a trip for fun."

Her hands in fists, Odile stalked back into the dormitory. "I'll ask Papa!"

The following day, when Slainie went to see the sisters off, Odile was nestled in the back of the wagon.

Sister Adele smiled. "She helped us load all of our provisions and has been convincing us all morning that we truly need her assistance for our journey."

As Sister Maggie placed a basket next to Odile, she smirked at Adele. There had obviously been talk amongst the three that Slainie hadn't been privy to.

Sister Maggie's smile abruptly changed. As she turned to Slainie, she spoke with a flat, sober tone. "You should come too. It will be good for both of you."

Realizing they had been inside the chapel fence for weeks, Slainie suddenly felt a spark of elation. *Why not?* If the burnt district was gruesome, she could shield Odile's eyes or keep her covered inside the wagon. Slainie sent one of the sisters to tell Joseph that they were leaving.

Slainie didn't know what to expect, but the landscape soon brought her to tears. Everything lay flattened and dead. Being free of vegetation before the fire, the trail remained visible as it ran through the soot. Along the trailside, the burnt roots of red pines, aspen, and sugar maples poked out of the ground where they had once grown sturdy toward the sun. In silence, the women recognized where cabins and barns and shops had once stood—the piles of ashes mounded higher and wider in these places. At most homesteads, the fire had raced on before consuming everything, leaving behind wood fragments now twisting in heaps of grey, white and black. Sometimes, though rarely, Slainie made out the shape of a bureau or a bed or a table.

With no barriers to hinder it, the wind whooshed full speed past Slainie's ears. Otherwise, she could have wondered if she had gone deaf. No crickets chirped. No cicadas buzzed. No dashing deer's tail streaked into the woods, no fox, no birds, chipmunks, or any animal that lived in the trees. Only the crisp wind rushing freely over the earth. As far as the eye could see, the fire had laid waste to the land until they came closer to Green Bay. Then, at the boundary of the burnt district, autumn trees studded the horizon. Slainie beamed and squeezed Odile, gazing at the orange and red leaves towering into the sky.

They rolled past a long log church with a bronze bell inside its steeple and the arched windows of the brick town hall. Having almost forgotten the world outside the chapel, each building they passed engrossed Slainie. Next to the church hung a wooden sign that she couldn't make out. Squinting as they passed, she recognized the image of a mortar and pestle skillfully burned into the wood. *Oh, the apothecary.* Cafés, hotels and taverns lined the street. As she gazed at residents going in and out of the cobbler's, the tailor's and the general store, her smile dropped. Aux Premier Belges didn't have most of these shops before the fire, and now it would be decades until the settlers could build the town up enough to attract such a large amount of traffic on Main Street.

As Odile bounced impatiently beside her, Slainie closed her eyes and named all the sounds she could hear. "I hear the jingling of bells. Am I correct? Can you see them?"

"Yes, Mama. There is a man with little cakes ringing his bell."

"Horses are whinnying also, and oxen are snorting . . . Oh, there are some birds twittering, too." Slainie sat tall and still as she perceived more sounds. "Pots clanging, most likely tied to the side of a wagon. And, a man is talking loudly and boastfully behind us . . . Now, two women are chattering . . . just over there . . .," Slainie pointed in the direction of their voices. "I hear some children laughing. It sounds like they—"

"They're quite funny!" Odile suddenly leaned over the sideboards on the wagon bed. "Look at them, Mama. That one's blindfolded." Worried that Odile might roll out of the wagon, Slainie quickly grabbed her legs. Across the street, a young boy ran blindfolded with both arms reaching out in front of him. Ten or so other children scattered in all directions as he tried to tag them.

A moment later, the wagon stopped in front of a beautiful white dolomite estate, the home of Mr. Cressy, the former Mayor of Green Bay. Shaded by triangular pines on either side, the large house boasted three chimneys. A dog sat panting on the upper deck beneath a stained-glass bullseye window. On the bottom stoop, a boy in red-tinted coveralls tied his shoe. *He must work in the meat packing factory.* Not even noticing them, he strolled past the wagon, smiling at his shoes the whole way to the street.

Two women conversed inside the open doorway. Slainie and the sisters slid past them. Odile sat in a tall-backed chair that looked like the plush throne of a queen. At one end of the parlor, Mrs. Cressy glided from the desk to the table to the cabinets and back again, all the while moving crates and shuffling papers. The room was in a state of chaos, but the woman's purposeful movements—and the tidy bun in her hair—said order existed somewhere in the mess.

Adele strolled to the desk. "Mrs. Elizabeth Cressy?"

"That I am," said the woman, smiling generously as she kept working.

"We would be most grateful for a minute to speak with you."

"Yes, do sit, and do *not* mind my bustling. I am listening. What are your needs?"

Sister Adele told Mrs. Cressy about the survivors who were now living at the chapel. Then Sister Maggie recited items from a long written list. After hearing this, Mrs. Cressy dropped a pile of papers on her desk and sat, her incessant motion ceasing with a loud creaking of her chair. She shifted her weight until she was comfortable and looked at the sisters with genuine concern.

"It seems you have quite a large flock under your care, and this miracle, as you call it, is truly an unexplainable stroke of luck.

It is absolutely within my means to provide you some assistance. You say you have the most immediate need of clothing, food, and bedding?"

Sister Adele folded her hands in her lap, the sleeves of her black habit bunching in the crooks of her elbows. "*Oui*. We do not have enough livestock to feed everyone we are housing."

Sister Maggie leaned toward the red mahogany desk. "We do have men who can work for themselves, though. Women, too."

Mrs. Cressy jotted something down with a fountain pen. "I can see about finding work for your people. For now, let us see what we can gather for you to take back today."

All around the house, baskets, bins, and bags cluttered tables and spilled out onto the floor. Mrs. Cressy had crammed her hutch with various bowls, cups and plates. Down the hallway, shoes sat in baskets, and in another room off the hallway, cozy-looking piles of bedding were stacked high. Odile bounded over to the door of the "bedding" room and Slainie whispered to her, "Darling, you must fight the urge to leap into those piles." Odile crossed her arms and trudged back to her chair. Sister Maggie peered slyly at Odile, as if to say she wanted to leap into those piles, too.

Naming items, Mrs. Cressy pointed to different areas of the house. The sisters began moving donations out to the porch. Slainie and Odile went to work in the wagon, shuffling the crates and bags around so everything would fit. An old man walked up the path and Slainie paused. He darted inside the house and emerged with his burly arms around a stack of crates. Whenever the sisters tried to bring anything down the steps, he relieved them of their burdens. After handing the last crate to Slainie, he asked Sister Adele to hear his confession. Smiling, she told him he ought to go to the priest to make his confession. Then, with a finger, she drew a cross on his forehead and said a prayer with him instead.

When there wasn't an inch of the wagon bed left to fill, Slainie took Odile back inside the house to bid farewell to Mrs. Cressy.

"Where did you get all of these?" asked Odile, pointing to the baskets of shoes in the hallway.

Mrs. Cressy adoringly smoothed Odile's hair. "Everywhere, my dear. From people in Wisconsin, and across the country—even some from Canada. I get more each day. It's a wonder that we receive so much, given the great need caused by fires in Chicago and Michigan as well. Come, I'll show you a letter."

She rounded her desk and pulled out a long envelope labeled with swooping calligraphy. She unwound the string at the top, removed a letter and read it aloud:

Dear Madam,

Through the Tribune I have obtained your name as someone hoping to relieve the needs of the "little ones" who are sufferers by the forest fires. Enclosed please find one dollar as a New Year's present from my infant class. My class is the youngest at the school, and as German children constitute one third of the class, I consider it quite a liberal sum for them. The class noted that this dollar should be given to a little girl to buy her whatever she most needs. No doubt you could spend one hundred dollars instead of one hundred cents in aiding the poor children, and I wish it were in my power to send you a large amount of money. Is it asking too much to request that you write me a note that I may read to my class to tell them how you spent the money, and what the little girl, whoever she is, said on receiving the gift? In this way, I may be able to interest the children to contribute more from time to time.

Yours with respect,
Mrs. E. H. Sears – Collinsville, Connecticut.

Trembling, Sister Maggie set her hand on Slainie's arm, smiling through tears. Mrs. Cressy read another letter:

> *As a mother, my heart yearns especially towards suffering children, and nothing could give me greater happiness than what little I am able to send to those destitute little ones.*

A hundred dollars came from Ed L. Baker, Esquire in Boston. The treasurer from a ladies' sewing club had raised $32.65. Ten came from the capitol, where Mrs. Cressy said most of the aid was being collected.

There were letters *seeking* aid, too. One pleaded on behalf of a mother of eight who also had an ill husband. Even Wisconsin Governor Lucius Fairchild had written letters, finishing one of them with: *I trust God in His mercy will rule it all in the end for His glory, though it is hard to see through the trials now.*

Slainie didn't think Mrs. Cressy was a religious woman. She didn't seem moved by the sentiment that God had a hand in any of this. No religious statues or images decorated her home, as one might imagine in a home as lavish as hers. Instead, a carved triangle with a large "G" in the middle seemed to have the position of prominence in the study. *A Freemason.* Slainie had seen it somewhere before and intuitively knew it wasn't a symbol for God.

Mrs. Cressy looked at Odile. "So, what do you say?"

Odile looked back, confused.

"What shall I tell the teacher in Connecticut about the little girl who received the dollar from her students?" Mrs. Cressy withdrew the money from an envelope and handed it to Odile.

Odile stared bright-eyed at the coins in her hand. She probably wanted to buy some candy with it, because she hadn't had a sweet morsel since before the fire.

To Slainie's surprise, Odile looked up and said, "A crib."
The three women smiled at each other. Standing proudly, Odile
lifted her chin. "For the babies, because there are so many in the
schoolhouse."

Mrs. Cressy nodded. "You may not find a crib for a dollar.
How about a rattle or two for the babies to play with? I think you
will have enough for a few from Kramer's. It's just"—Mrs. Cressy
gestured toward the street—"down this road, right at Pearl Street
and up three."

Mrs. Cressy handed Odile two more dollars and said, "Buy
Kramer's big bag of cream sweeties as well, but remember, you
must be certain to hand them out one by one and make sure every
child has one. You can uplift them, give them fighting spirit."

Gazing up at Slainie, Odile pleaded with angelic eyes. Slainie
nodded, and Odile closed her fist tightly around the money. Mrs.
Cressy told them to return the following week for another load
of donations.

On the ride home, Odile snuggled into a pile of bedding with
a big bag of Kramer's cream sweeties in her lap. Slainie and Odile
shook the baby rattles while the sisters sang hymns the whole way.
When they pulled up to the burnt side of the chapel fence, people
came to help unload, shouting the names of available items. "Who
needs socks?" "Overcoats?" "Flannel shirts?" "Quilts?" "A boy's
vest?" "A calico dress?" People raised their hands and stepped to
the front of the crowd when they heard something they needed.
With so many donated items, this auction of sorts continued for
over an hour. When everything was gone, Sister Adele assured
everyone that more was coming soon.

CHAPTER TWENTY

New Life

AS SLAINIE STOOD inside the empty wagon bed, the crowd began to dissipate. Throwing on their new coats and scarves, the cold settlers moseyed back to the campfires. A group of children wrestled to pull new dresses and pants over their clothing, too excited to wait until they reached private quarters for changing. Others toddled around in wooden clogs too big for their feet. As Odile dashed from child to child, she gave each one a cream sweetie. Slainie's heart swelled as she watched them all, happy and zestful, like they had just been served a bowl of warm hope. It seemed everyone at the chapel had something new that they had needed.

As Slainie handed out the last of the blankets, she noticed her mother hauling food boxes into the dormitory. Something seemed different about her. Her face appeared *lifted*—her eyes, her cheeks, the corners of her mouth. She seemed lighter. Slainie finally recognized it, for she had seen this change before; it was joy. Oh, how her mother moved with cheeriness and grace among the settlers in the yard.

Wanting to talk to her, Slainie stepped away from the wagon to follow her inside. Odile ran up, babbling about the reactions of each child she'd given a sweetie to. Her smile glowed with the soft glimmer of campfires. Witnessing Odile's exuberant facial expressions, Slainie's heart burst with gratitude. Instead of going to find her mother, she felt compelled to sit on the ground with Odile and listen to her lively retelling.

Realizing that she hadn't kept up with her family and friends at all, Slainie made a mental note that she *would* need to speak with her mother later. Everyone was so busy helping the sisters teach and tend children, care for livestock, build winter huts from half-burned logs, or scavenge for food and supplies. Re-settling their burnt land was every bit as difficult as settling the land in the first place. In fact, it had even more challenges—there was no land to settle, no trees with which to build, no wild foods growing, and no wild animals to hunt. Many of the survivors weren't as lucky as Slainie—many had also lost family and friends in the flames. At least she had a support system, and that meant a much smaller hole in her heart.

That evening, after Sophie and Odile were asleep, Slainie stepped outside with Joseph. A November chill bit her cheeks and she pulled her new quilt tight around her shoulders. They walked toward the campfires where Mr. Lafont sat with some of his friends. Lingering behind him, they looked down at the burning logs. It seemed strange—this chemical reaction that devoured her entire settlement was also the most essential means of cooking, heating, and even disinfecting. Yet, fire still made Slainie uneasy—that orange and red glow—even contained in a pit.

"Evening, Papa."

"Evening to you, *ma chérie*." Mr. Lafont turned his head. "Ah. Evening, Joseph." He made room for them to sit on his blanket.

Slainie leaned into her father, resting her head on his shoulder, and the three of them went back to staring silently at the flames.

"How are the babies?" Mr. Lafont finally asked.

"They are well. They have it better than most children here. Odile is making friends, and Sophie is happy as long as she is with me. They are not so much different than they were before."

"Good. Good. I wish these days gave us more time to play."

"It is not a problem, Papa. They have a lot of other children to play with."

"I miss home. Do you miss home?" asked Mr. Lafont.

"*Ouais*, every day." Slainie sighed and glanced at Joseph.

Joseph placed his hand on hers. "We will soon have a new one, as comfortable as the last."

Slainie closed her eyes and envisioned Sophie and Odile scampering on their old wooden floors, laughter filling the house. When sadness swept over her, she shook the memory away.

"I thought I would visit with mother tonight. Where is she?"

Her father raised an arm toward the chapel. "I am not sure. She has been going off at dusk—over there."

A lantern flickered through the chapel door.

"No. There, 'round back." He pointed into darkness. "She is gone for hours and says she is behind the chapel. She comes back in a fine mood, so I leave her be."

"Hmm." Slainie kissed Joseph's cheek and stood. "I will go look for her."

Leaving the light of the campfires, she ran a hand along the rough outer wall of the chapel.

"Mother?" she whispered, afraid to make a sound. "Mother?"

She inched slowly around the corner, letting her eyes adjust to the darkness beyond the chapel. Her mother sat on the ground, barely illuminated by the flame of a single candle.

"Mother? It is so dark back here. Are you all right? What are you doing?"

"Slainie!" Mrs. Lafont started, nearly extinguishing her flame.

Slainie sat down at a distance. She couldn't see Mrs. Lafont's face well enough to tell if the interruption angered or gladdened her. Knowing her mother had never enjoyed small talk, she made haste to her point.

"How have you been?"

"Me? I have been well, considering where we are." Mrs. Lafont wrung her hands.

"I have seen you around, helping everyone, working and keeping busy . . . but we have not had a chance to talk since . . . well, we have not talked in a long time."

With the candle in between them, the darkness shrouded half of Mrs. Lafont's face. The hair on her lit side glowed a warm auburn. "I have a knack for being busy, and it is a good thing to have around here. Someone is always making a new request for help. My talent for being busy had never been tested before!"

Was that a joke? Slainie made out a smile on her mother's face and realized she might be approaching her mother too timidly. She smiled back.

"I think you *are* helping a good bit, and you look happy. I am sure something is different about you."

"Maybe, but I can't speak about it." Lowering her arms, Mrs. Lafont drew the light away from her face. Slainie looked away, feeling discouraged.

"That is not what I meant. I mean, I don't think I have *the words* to speak about it."

Slainie turned back. "Why not?"

"How do I describe it? I have no idea how I have changed. I just have."

"You know, I never asked you how you got here. I mean, you came alone during the fire . . . without Papa."

"Your father told me that you tried to come for me," said Mrs. Lafont. "Of course, I am glad you did not come—it was horrible out there—but I like knowing you would have."

"I would have, Maman. Of course I would have."

"When your father left with Modette, I was obviously scared. I was all alone in the house. I knew I should have gone with them, but I was angry. Stubborn. I did not want to leave. But I started for the chapel anyway. I saw your father on the trail and grabbed hold of him, but he told me to go on. He stayed behind to help some elders struggling to keep pace against the fire. It was horrendous on those trails. Loud and dark, but for that terrible red glow ahead. We were running toward it. I knew it, but I just ran. There was no time to go anywhere else. I trampled over others who fell in the way—I did not mean to. They fell under me, and I just ran."

Slainie leaned toward her mother, but stopped, unsure if she would accept a hug. Surprisingly, Mrs. Lafont pulled Slainie into her arms and began to sob.

"I did not want to die. I thought I wanted to. I had wanted to for so long." The words gushed out of her. "Ever since Cecilia died, I did not have the will to live. All I felt was bitterness."

"I know . . . I know. I knew this," said Slainie.

"I have been angry for years. Cruel." Mrs. Lafont put her hands on Slainie's shoulders, pushing her back. She looked in her eyes. "You were right to leave me. You were always right. I just could not admit it to you."

Slainie didn't know what to say. This type of honesty and humility from her mother was unexpected. As she wondered if she could trust it, tears welled in her eyes. By the time they streamed to her chin, she had forgiven her mother for everything. Her chest expanded with a deep inhalation. Then her shoulders relaxed, and she clung to her mother again.

"You did love me," she murmured, feeling full inside where there had been emptiness. She ached to burst out with everything her mother had missed about her conversion and her life now.

Her mother wiped Slainie's cheeks with her thumbs. "I never listened to you or your father."

"You had no belief in God, so why would you have listened?" Slainie gazed at the small circle of light cast by the dainty candle on the ground.

"That is not why I did not listen. I believed there was a God. I just could not talk to Him. I could not look at Him. To me, God was a murderer. The God that I had been told loved me had let this horrible thing happen to my precious daughter. I did not believe He loved me, so I was not going to love Him either."

"That is terrible." Slainie couldn't imagine being that angry at God, so angry you'd refuse to even try to talk to Him.

"I do not know that I will ever understand why Cecilia had to die. I am still her mother, and it still makes me angry. Here, at the chapel now, I have been listening to all this talk of miracles. I heard Father Peter's story. I am not certain of anything, but I am starting to see how much God has done for us and all the things He has given us."

"Blessings," said Slainie.

"I see them now. God let me keep you and Modette and your brothers. You are all blessings. We had a home, and we can say we earned our place in America. We have survived where many died trying, even before the fire. But, really, it was Odile who first made me feel this way. Sweet Odile. She is so much like your sister, Cecilia. When she was born, I felt your sister again. Then, Sophie came, and I looked forward to something. I wanted to see both of them every day."

Slainie struggled against the urge to sob again. So many emotions rushed through her. She wanted to share them all, but she didn't want her mother to stop talking. Then she noticed the circle of stones next to the candle in front of them.

"What are these rocks? Did *you* put them here?"

"Yes, I did. A few days ago."

Slainie picked one up and brushed a finger across it. Her mother reached for it, and Slainie placed it in her hand. "What are they for?"

"They are for Cecilia." Mrs. Lafont took out a small rag and polished the stone before returning it to the circle.

Slainie finally saw it. *A grave.*

"It is my place to speak to her. I always regretted leaving her alone in Kaukauna," said Mrs. Lafont.

"So did I."

Even as she recalled her little sister's body being lowered into the ground, joy surged. *We are talking . . . not just talking, but we are sharing Cecilia.* This was the unfulfilled hope that had driven Slainie from her parents' home when she was eighteen. Now here they were. It wasn't the kitchen table set with plates and flowers and a surprise pie, but even sitting behind the chapel in the dark, this was an accomplishment.

Silence washed over them. Her mother tidied the circle by brushing back a growing rim of dirt around the stones and plucking up the fall leaves wedged in between them. Slainie let her mind wander to better memories of Cecilia.

"Remember when she tied bows around all of the boxes in our hut? I remember she used your thread and some twine from beef we bought at the market."

Her mother leaned back and laughed. "She said she was turning everything into a present for me. She used whatever she could find. She never lacked for something to do. Artistic, that child was."

"She gave me one too. When I opened it, I was disappointed. There were only spices inside. I should have known. The box was your spice box, only with something like a bow tied around it."

Again they stared down at the circle of stones. Slainie liked the idea of having a place for remembering Cecilia, a grave for her. A place, even, for Odile and Sophie to meet their aunt someday.

A voice came from behind them. "Good evening."

Slainie startled, but Mrs. Lafont didn't flinch. A figure came closer in the darkness carrying a lantern.

"There is someone else with you this time, Mrs. Lafont?"

Recognizing the voice as Sister Adele's, Slainie stood to greet her.

"Good evening, Sister." After embracing, they sat near the stones.

"Mother, were you expecting Sister?"

"Yes."

For a moment, they were all quiet, and Slainie was confused. *Did Sister Adele always stroll alone behind the chapel in the dead of night?*

Clarity struck. "You have been teaching her!"

Sister Adele laughed softly. "I have been."

"Maman, this is wonderful. This is amazing."

Raising her hands, Mrs. Lafont patted the air. "Slow down, Slainie. I am no saint yet. I have been talking to God, yes, but I still do not agree with Him on everything."

"Of course not, but you will come to understand," said Slainie.

"Maybe, and maybe not. I do not have to agree with everything I am told."

Hearing her mother's mood sour, Slainie felt a familiar frustration.

Sister Adele spoke in a hushed, sympathetic tone. "Give your mother some time. God has used the fire to touch many hearts, but the fire has not only opened hearts. It has confused some also. You know well that suffering is not an easy way to learn."

Mrs. Lafont's voice softened, too. "Like I said, I am talking to God, but I still do not like all the destruction and death He has caused."

Slainie tilted her head and peered at her mother. "Caused?"

"That is what we have been discussing the last few days," said Sister Adele. "I have been explaining to your mother the difference between God *causing* a bad thing to happen and God *allowing* bad to happen."

"Do you think God caused this fire?" Slainie asked her mother.

Mrs. Lafont turned to Adele, her pale face shining brightly in the flickering lantern flame. "Wasn't it Mary who warned us when she appeared? Adele, you said she told you there would be a chastisement."

"Yes, but she did not say the Lord would *cause* it," said Sister Adele. "Men could have caused it by leaving piles of sawdust in the sun. The world doesn't exist in perfect harmony. Wind and sun and rain do not always work to man's benefit."

"You have always told me that God is good, all good, and that He can never do anything evil," said Slainie.

"That is correct. I *have* told you this; however, you mistake a fire as evil. A fire is not necessarily an evil, though a fire and the destruction it causes are the result of evil—the first sin altered the perfect balance of man *and* nature."

Mrs. Lafont clicked her tongue and groaned. "We have spoken about this over and over. We keep going round, and it still does not make sense to me."

"Maman, be patient." Hesitantly, Slainie put her hand on Mrs. Lafont's back, relieved when her mother didn't shrug it off.

"Are you going to keep meeting with Adele? I mean, often?"

"*I* hope so," said Sister Adele.

Mrs. Lafont nodded slowly. "I have enjoyed it."

When the conversation didn't pick up again, Slainie thought her presence might be preventing her mother from speaking openly with Sister Adele. After all, they had this meeting scheduled before Slainie ever showed up.

"I am going to go." Slainie unfolded her legs. "I think . . . I think that I should go check on the girls." She stood and stretched her back. "Umm . . . I love you, Maman."

Mrs. Lafont's hand suddenly shot up. Uncharacteristically, she squeezed Slainie's hand and didn't let go.

"Good night, Sister," Slainie said to Adele, hesitating for a moment. Mrs. Lafont hadn't released her hand.

"I . . . love you too," Mrs. Lafont said. "I always have." She let Slainie's hand slip out of her grip.

Awkwardly, Slainie stumbled through the darkness until she felt the chapel wall beneath her fingers. She couldn't wait to tell Joseph about this. Her father would cry when he heard. She groped her way along the cold wood, moving toward the little huddles of people in the chapel yard.

Her steps were heavy, as if a magnet were pulling her back toward her mother. She wanted to return to the circle of stones and talk all night long. A surge of energy made her want to jump and skip. Instead, she paused to collect herself, leaning against the wall, and closed her eyes. She squeezed in all the hopes and all the joy like a hug and released them in a prayer. *I trust you, Lord. Let Mary take care of her. Let Adele guide her.* Then she gently released the burden of saving her mother from her heart.

Taking one blind step after another, Slainie continued through the darkness, with only the chapel wall to guide her. The immovable sanctuary set her feet on a straight path like a compass. She braced herself against it to ensure she was moving in the right direction. Full of confidence and peace, she soon spotted the little campfires dotting the yard. When the chapel wall ended, she confidently let go and stepped into the glow.

"I have rejoiced in what has been said to me.
We shall enter the house of the Lord."

Sister Adele on her deathbed.
July 5th, 1896
66 years old

AFTERWORD

THE IDEA TO write a book based on Our Lady of Good Help (OLGH) came to me after two visits to Champion Shrine in Wisconsin. There my husband and I had two petitions answered. One precipitated a move to a new country. The other is our now six-year-old son.

Our prayers answered, we owed patronage to OLGH, so I printed and laminated prayer cards for my family. We moved again, this time intending to plant roots in California. That's where the urge to write resurfaced.

Three years had passed since our visits to the Shrine, and I was still fascinated with the idea of Adele Brise trekking through the wilderness with her message. I couldn't get this scene out of my head — a girl sewing in a chair in a cabin with her mother. Hearing a knock, they open the front door to find a mysterious stranger with a missing eye: Adele.

So I had one scene.

Plus, I had prayer, which led to my belief that this is what Our Lady wanted me to write about.

I also had a master's in journalism and a love for writing.

But I had no idea what I was doing.

I quickly learned that I am lucky to write stories in the 21st century. Why? Well, the Internet. Even though I had visited the Shrine twice, I didn't have experience with Belgium, pioneering, losing a child, or riding in a wagon for days.

There was a time when novelists had to travel, take odd or dangerous jobs, or spend years living among the subjects they wrote about. For example, the great American novelist Ernest Hemingway crafted his novels about bull fighting after his time living in Spain. As a young man, he was wounded driving a Red Cross ambulance during WWI, and he was also a war reporter during the Spanish Civil War; both experiences were funneled into his legendary novel *For Whom the Bell Tolls.*

With the Internet, I was able to read accounts from immigrants making the ocean voyage to America. I was able to study hand-drawn maps of New York Harbor in the 1800s. I found the plants and people native to Wisconsin. I learned about Belgium and what drove the Walloons to come to America. I read many free out-of-print books. I also found people who were willing to correspond with me over a period of years and share what they had or what they knew.

Luckily, my characters are part of the largest group of Belgians in America. They are the subject of many dissertations, novels, websites, and museums. As the largest in American history, the fire in my story is also the subject of many writings and has its own museum. The Peshtigo Fire Museum was created in 1963 and is located in Peshtigo, WI.

My characters are based on historical accounts of the first Belgians to settle in Wisconsin. My account of Adele Brise stayed closer to fact than any other characters I wrote about. Her father, mother, two sisters and herself are recorded as members of the party of Belgians to arrive in 1855. As a child, Adele was injured in an accident involving the chemical lye and lost her eye. According to historical accounts, Adele did make a promise with her friends at their First Holy Communion to become missionaries and serve poor children. Not wanting to leave Belgium for this reason, she visited her pastor who, as mentioned in my book, advised her to obey her parents.

I felt it was important to stick to the official, recorded story of Adele Brise and the apparition of the Virgin Mary. For this reason, my book describes the apparition exactly as it has been recorded by the Archdiocese of Green Bay. Adele's conversations, however, and the description of her farmhouse had to be invented. Sadly, we have so little record of her personal life.

My other characters are composites of fact and fiction. Mr. Lafont is based on a man named Philippe Hannon, who voyaged to Brown County in 1853 with the first wave of Belgians to settle the area. He was swindled in New York by the Strauss Shipping Company. He left his family behind in Green Bay, WI, while he searched with a group of men for land to purchase. Sadly, while he was away, his youngest child died. Because the Belgians had to wait in Green Bay to bury Hannon's child, Father Daems chanced to meet them and convinced them to build where Champion, WI, is today. Father Daems is a real man who came to America as a missionary. Later, he was sent to Adele's chapel to investigate her and her story.

Another character, Pauline, is based on one of the few people who preserved and retold the apparition story in real life. Pauline LaPlante learned from Adele and later became a Franciscan Sister in Green Bay, taking over at the chapel when Adele died. Sister Maggie (Marguerite) was a teacher at Adele's school. There was also a large family that included a Joseph, a Marguerite and a Sophie with a home near the chapel. Even the name of each teacher at Adele's school was taken from historical accounts.

Reverend Peter Pernin's story of surviving the Peshtigo Fire was summarized, but that *is* his story. To write it, I used the book *The Finger of God Was There!* by Reverend P. Pernin, 1874. The miraculous tabernacle that he mentioned is on display at the Peshtigo Fire Museum to this day. Xavier Martin (Marie's brother) is also a real person, who stayed behind in Philadelphia to learn English before joining the Belgians in Wisconsin and leading them to active civil and political life.

To bring to life the immense relief efforts after the Peshtigo Fire, I used real letters. The letters read by Mrs. Cressy are from the collection *Henry and Elizabeth Baird Papers, 1798-1937* that are archived at the Wisconsin Historical Society. Henry was the former mayor of Green Bay and his wife did coordinate fire relief efforts for the region.

There are kernels of the past woven into every sentence in this book, but what I couldn't find, I had to describe somehow and hope that I was being true to history. I leaned on prayer and guidance from Our Lady for these parts.

(As an aside, Champion Shrine is also known as The National Shrine of Our Lady of Good Help. The town of Champion has also gone by the name of Robinsonville.)

Below is an incomplete list of resources I am grateful for:

Personal narratives from important figures in the history of Wisconsin, such as *The Belgians of Northeast Wisconsin* (Xavier Martin, Wisconsin Historical Society) and *The Finger of God Was There!* (Rev. Peter Pernin, no copyright).

The Wisconsin Historical Society and University of Wisconsin-Madison Libraries.

Google images to build out the world in my story. For example, Vincent Van Gogh was Belgian and was from the same province as Adele. He was born the year she left for America. His paintings of Belgium were most helpful in describing the life of my characters as Belgian peasants.

Jacqueline Lee Tinkler's thesis "The Walloons Immigrants of Northeast Wisconsin" at the University of Texas Arlington. Her research is incredibly broad and detailed, and she was very kind.

The books *Growing Up in the Country* (Elliot West) and *The First Book of Pioneers* (Walter Havighurst, 1959 edition).

On the Water Exhibition (online) of the Smithsonian National Museum of American History, Rootsweb.com, Ancestry.com, and Wikipedia (which is always ONLY a starting point in any research subject).

ACKNOWLEDGMENTS

THE PEOPLE TO whom I am most grateful:

My husband, who has given me approximately 1,200 hours to write. I know the stress it has caused you, watching movies alone at night, wrangling our kids, telling me the truth even when it angered me, and listening to me obsess for probably the same number of hours. You always steer me true!

My kids, for dealing with a mommy who is so often preoccupied. For inspiring me. You have been proud of your mom, and that's really special.

My friend, Kat Hnatiuk, for transforming this book and holding my hand as I was rejected by a half dozen Catholic publishers. Thank you for months of editing with me and hours chatting online about ideas and life issues.

Sister Agnes Fischer, the archivist with the Sisters of Saint Francis of the Holy Cross in Green Bay, WI. You spent hours collecting research for me and responding to frequent questions over email. I hope someday to meet you.

Corrie Campbell, the communications coordinator at the Champion Shrine. One night back in 2018, I sent you an unpolished draft of the story. When you called the next morning to gush about how much you liked it, I cried. You devoured it in one night! You have been so supportive and gave me hope when it was hard to keep writing.

My friend, Dara. You once pointed to a shelf in your house and said, "That's the shelf I put good books about saints on. Hopefully, yours will go right *there* when it's finished." You read the book twice all the way through to comment and eliminate typos, while your four kids screamed and played around you. You always believed in me. (Also, you introduced me to Kat.)

To another editor (and author), Carolyn Astfalk. You taught me how to use better verbs, write with an active voice, eliminate pet words, and cut redundancies. For always being happy to help and sharing my novel with your girls!

Sally Thomas, who showed me a better way to structure the story and how to create vivid settings. She also answers my homeschooling questions with great detail and wisdom.

To Abby the Great, Marisa the Pierson, Ann at the Beach, Catholic Mum, Chris Lewis, Kendra Tierney, and Mary who is Meant To Fly—you know who you are and what you've done to help me with this book.

To my beta readers, the kids who took the time to read this book and be put on the spot. Thanks for your honesty!

To my mother and grandmother, who have been proud of everything I have ever accomplished, even when it's mediocre. Sometimes you just need one person who always believes you can achieve your dreams. I was blessed with quite a few.

To all of my family and friends who don't ascribe to Christian beliefs yet were enthusiastic about my work anyway.

To God, my Father in heaven, thank you for using my gifts in the completion of Your will. Thank you for all the blessings you give me and my family.

To Mama Mary, for being the perfect mother. For coming to Wisconsin to teach us and give us hope. For leading my whole family toward peace through this apparition—and always toward your Son.

To Jesus, my Lord, for Your gentle guidance, forgiveness, discipline, death, and resurrection. For the wisdom of Your divine plan. Nothing matters without You.

DECREE ON THE AUTHENTICITY OF THE APPARITION OF 1859 AT THE SHRINE OF OUR LADY OF GOOD HELP DIOCESE OF GREEN BAY BISHOP DAVID RICKEN

December 8, 2010

GIVEN THAT

For over one hundred fifty-one years, a continuous flow of the faithful has come to Champion, Wisconsin to pray, to seek solace and comfort in times of trouble and to petition Our Lord Jesus Christ through the powerful intercession to Our Lady of Good Help.

Incessant prayer has gone up in this place based upon the word of a young Belgian immigrant woman, Adele Brise, who in October 1859 said that the Blessed Mother, a Lady clothed in dazzling white, had appeared to her on this site.

The Lady was elevated slightly in a bright light and gave words of solace and comfort and a bold and challenging mission for the young immigrant woman. The Lady gave her a two-fold mission of prayer for the conversion of sinners and catechesis. "I am the Queen of Heaven who prays for the conversion of sinners, and I wish you to do the same. You received Holy Communion this morning and that is well. But you must do more. Make a

general confession and offer Communion for the conversion of
sinners. . . . Gather the children in this wild country and teach
them what they should know for salvation. . . . Teach them their
catechism, how to sign themselves with the sign of the Cross, and
how to approach the sacraments; that is what I wish you to do. Go
and fear nothing, I will help you."

Adele Brise began immediately to fulfill the mandate and
mission entrusted to her by the Lady and oftentimes at great personal sacrifice went to the homes of the children to instruct them
in the largely unsettled and forested area in Wisconsin. Adele was
ever obedient to the authorities of the Church and steadfast in the
mission entrusted to her by Our Lady, no matter what difficulty
she encountered.

The mission given her became such a commitment that she
set up a Catholic school of instruction for children and even began
a community of Third Order Franciscan women, who assisted her
in her obedience to the mandate of Our Lady to pray for the conversion of sinners and to instruct the children.

A long tradition of oral and some documented sources
recounting answered prayers at the Shrine of Our Lady of Good
Help include conversions and many physical healings attributed
to the Blessed Mother's intercession. Many physical healings are
memorialized by the multitude of crutches and other mementoes
of thanksgiving for answered prayers left at the Shrine. Prayers for
physical healing are answered even to this day through the intercession of Our Lady of Good Help. Though none of these favors
have been officially declared a miracle by the Church, they are
clear evidence of spiritual fruitfulness and the history of devotion
to the Blessed Virgin Mary at the Shrine.

Graces have been poured out through the sacraments cel-
ebrated in this place especially through the celebration of the
Mass and the Sacrament of Reconciliation, as well as through the

recitation of public devotions and private prayers.

Our Lady has lessened or relieved the burdens of the People of God, whether about financial, familial, relationship or employment matters or even through diminishing inclement and tempestuous weather.

This holy place was preserved from the infamous Peshtigo fire of 1871, when many of the faithful gathered here with Adele and prayed through the intercession of Our Lady of Good Help, with the result that the fire that devastated everything in its wake in this entire area stopped when it reached the parameters of the Shrine.

There is clear testimony to the upright character of Adele Brise, her devotion to Jesus Christ and the Blessed Virgin Mary, and her unwavering commitment to the mission Mary entrusted to her. Moreover, the uninterrupted history of faith and devotion testifies to the spiritual fruits bestowed upon the pilgrims to the Shrine.

GIVEN ALL OF THE ABOVE

Three Marian experts have studied the history of this alleged apparition and all of the extant documents, letters, and written testimonies in order to determine whether or not there are inherent contradictions or objections to the veracity of the testimony given by Adele Brise with regard to the events of 1859 and to establish whether or not there is enough evidence to suggest that the events which happened to Adele Brise may be of a supernatural origin. The accounts of the apparitions and locutions are judged to be free from doctrinal error and consistent with the Catholic faith. There is nothing in the person and character of Adele Brise that would question the veracity of the substance of her account. In fact, her personal character is a major factor in favor of the recognition of the apparition.

Objections concerning whether there was enough evidence to support a judgment in favor of the supernatural character of the events were thoroughly investigated and answered by the experts. The documents from the early history of the Shrine are not abundant, due primarily to the fact that Green Bay at the time of the apparition was frontier country. One of the experts affirmed that any lack of information does "not invalidate the overall impression of coherence between event and consequences, personality of the seer and commitment to the mission received, the comparability between this event and similar recognized apparitions, and challenges of the historical context and responses given."

GIVEN THAT

These simple apparitions and locutions given to Adele Brise became such a compelling theological and religious mission for her. The effects of these endeavors by her and many others have lasted these many years with such major spiritual benefit to so many people.

Many of the local clergy and clergy from other Dioceses and Religious Institutes have come here on pilgrimage with their people, also with spiritual benefit.

If you would like to know more about the factual people and events in this novel visit **www.theonibell.com**. You can also visit the official website for the Shrine at **www.championshrine.org**.